THE INCREDIBLE JOURNEY

"Captivating! A tale of charm, high drama and some revelations of the love existing between man and beast."
The New York Times

"An incredible book! A beautiful story so moving that it stays in the mind constantly. It is a gem to be treasured!"
The St. Louis Post-Dispatch

"I have read THE INCREDIBLE JOURNEY with much enjoyment. Obviously the author has a great knowledge of animals and a great love for them."
**Joy Adamson,
author of BORN FREE**

ANNE OF GREEN GABLES by L.M. Montgomery
THE DOG WHO WOULDN'T BE by Farley Mowat
GOODBYE, MR. CHIPS by James Hilton
NEVER CRY WOLF by Farley Mowat
THE RED PONY by John Steinbeck
ROLL OF THUNDER, HEAR MY CRY by Mildred D. Taylor
VERY FAR AWAY FROM ANYWHERE ELSE by
  Ursula K. LeGuin
WHEN THE LEGENDS DIE by Hal Borland
WHERE THE RED FERN GROWS by Wilson Rawls
INCIDENT AT HAWK'S HILL by Allan W. Eckert

The Incredible Journey

by Sheila Burnford

with illustrations by Carl Burger

BANTAM BOOKS

NEW YORK · TORONTO · LONDON · SYDNEY · AUCKLAND

*This low-priced Bantam Book
has been completely reset in a typeface
designed for easy reading, and was printed
from new plates. It contains the complete
text of the original hard-cover edition.*
NOT ONE WORD HAS BEEN OMITTED.

RL 6, IL age 11 and up

THE INCREDIBLE JOURNEY

*A Bantam Book / published by arrangement with
Little, Brown & Company, Inc. in association with
The Atlantic Monthly Press*

PRINTING HISTORY

*Little, Brown edition published March 1961
Eleven printings through 1962*

Condensation appeared in MCCALLS *Magazine March 1961*

Book-of-the-Month Club edition published April 1962

*Bantam edition / September 1961
Five printings through January 1963
New Bantam edition / November 1963
Five printings through April 1964
Bantam Pathfinder edition / April 1965
33 printings through April 1975
Bantam edition / October 1975
54 printings through June 1986*

*Starfire Books and accompanying logo of a stylized star
are registered trademarks of Bantam Books, Inc.*

ISBN 0-553-26218-1

Published simultaneously in the United States and Canada

PRINTED IN THE UNITED STATES OF AMERICA

O   74   73   72   71   70   69   68   67   66   65   64

THE BEASTS

I think I could turn and live with animals, they are so
  placid and self-contain'd,
I stand and look at them long and long.
They do not sweat and whine about their condition,
They do not lie awake in the dark and weep for their
  sins,
They do not make me sick discussing their duty to
  God
Not one is dissatisfied, not one is demented with the
  mania of owning things,
Not one kneels to another, nor to his kind that lived
  thousands of years ago,
Not one is respectable or industrious over the whole
  earth.

—WALT WHITMAN, *Leaves of Grass*, "Song of Myself,"
  32.

The Incredible Journey

1

THIS JOURNEY took place in a part of Canada which lies in the northwestern part of the great sprawling province of Ontario. It is a vast area of deeply wooded wilderness — of endless chains of lonely lakes and rushing rivers. Thousands of miles of country roads, rough timber lanes, overgrown tracks leading to abandoned mines, and unmapped trails snake across its length and breadth. It is a country of far-flung, lonely farms and a few widely scattered small towns and villages, of lonely trappers' shacks and logging camps. Most of its industry comes from the great pulp and paper companies who work their timber concessions deep in the very heart of the forests; and from the mines, for it is rich in minerals. Prospectors work through it; there are trappers and Indians; and sometimes hunters who fly into the virgin lakes in small amphibious aircraft; there are pioneers with visions beyond their own life span; and there are those who have left the bustle of civilization forever, to sink their identity in an unquestioning acceptance of the wilderness. But all these human beings together are as a handful of sand upon the ocean shores, and for the most part there is silence and solitude and an uninterrupted way of life for the wild animals that abound there: moose and deer, brown and black bears; lynx and fox; beaver, muskrat and otter; fishers, mink and marten. The wild duck rests there and the Canada goose, for this is a fringe of the central migratory flyway. The clear tree-fringed lakes and rivers are filled with speckled trout and steelheads, pike and pickerel and whitefish.

Almost half the year the country is blanketed with snow; and for weeks at a time the temperature may stay many degrees below zero; there is no slow growth of spring, but a sudden short burst of summer when everything grows with wild abandon; and as suddenly it is the fall again. To many who live there, fall is the burnished crown of the year, with the crisp sunny days and exhilarating air of the Northland; with clear blue skies, and drifting leaves, and, as far as the eye can see, the endless panorama of glorious rich flaming color in the turning trees.

This is the country over which the three travelers passed, and it was in the fall that they traveled, in the days of Indian summer.

John Longridge lived several miles from one of the small towns in an old stone house that had been in his family for several generations. He was a tall, austerely pleasant man of about forty, a bachelor, and a writer by profession, being the author of several historical biographies. He spent much of his time traveling and gathering material for his books, but always returned to the comfortable old stone house for the actual writing. He liked the house to himself during these creative periods, and for many years had enjoyed an ideal arrangement whereby his domestic wants were cared for by a middle-aged couple, Mrs. Oakes and her husband Bert, who lived in a small cottage about half a mile away. Mrs. Oakes came in every day to look after the house and cook the main meals. Bert was in charge of the furnace, the garden and all the odd jobs. They came and went about their business without disturbing Longridge, and there was complete accord among them all.

On the eve of the incredible journey, towards the end of September, Longridge sat by a crackling log fire in his comfortable library. The curtains were drawn and the firelight flickered and played on the bookshelves and danced on the ceiling. The only other light in the room came from a small shaded lamp on a table by the deep armchair. It was a very peaceful room and the only sound was the occasional crackling from the logs or the rustling of a newspaper, the pages of which Longridge turned with some difficulty, for a slender wheat-colored Siamese cat was curled on his knee, chocolate-colored front paws curved in towards one another, sapphire eyes blinking occasionally as he stared into the fire.

On the floor, his scarred, bony head resting on

one of the man's feet, lay an old white English bull terrier. His slanted almond-shaped eyes, sunk deep within their pinkish rims, were closed; one large triangular ear caught the firelight, flushing the inside a delicate pink, so that it appeared almost translucent. Anyone unaccustomed to the rather peculiar points of bull terrier beauty would have thought him a strange if not downright ugly dog, with the naked, down-faced arc of his profile, his deep-chested, stocky body and whip-tapered tail. But the true lover of an ancient and honorable breed would have recognized the blood and bone of this elderly and rather battered body; would have known that in his prime this had been a magnificent specimen of compact sinew and muscle, bred to fight and endure; and would have loved him for his curious mixture of wicked, unyielding fighter yet devoted and docile family pet, and above all for the irrepressible air of sly merriment which gleamed in his little slant eyes.

He twitched and sighed often in his sleep, as old dogs will, and for once his shabby tail with the bare patch on the last joint was still.

By the door lay another dog, nose on paws, brown eyes open and watchful in contrast to the peacefulness radiated by the other occupants of the room. This was a large red-gold Labrador retriever, a young dog with all the heritage of his sturdy working forebears in his powerful build, broad noble head and deep, blunt, gentle mouth. He lifted his head as Longridge rose from the chair, depositing the cat, with an apologetic pat, on the floor, and carefully moving his foot from under the old dog's head before walking across the room to draw one of the heavy curtains and look out.

A huge orange moon was rising just above the trees at the far end of the garden, and a branch of an old lilac tree tap-tapped in the light wind against the window pane. It was bright enough outside to see the garden in clear detail, and he noticed how the leaves had drifted again across the lawn even in the short time since it had been raked that afternoon, and that only a few brave asters remained to color the flower beds.

He turned and crossed the room, flicking on another light, and opened a narrow cupboard halfway up the wall. Inside were several guns on racks and he looked at them thoughtfully, running his fingers lovingly down the smooth grain of the hand-rubbed stocks, and finally lifted down a beautifully chased and engraved double-barreled gun. He "broke" it and peered down the gleaming barrels; and as though at a signal the young dog sat up silently in the shadows, his ears pricked in interest. The gun fell back into place with a well-oiled click and the dog whined. The man replaced the gun in sudden contrition, and the dog lay down again, his head turned away, his eyes miserable.

Longridge walked over to make amends for his thoughtlessness, but as he bent down to pat the dog the telephone rang so suddenly and shrilly in the quiet room that the cat jumped indignantly off the chair and the bull terrier started clumsily to his feet.

Longridge picked up the receiver, and presently the breathless voice of Mrs. Oakes was heard, accompanied by a high-pitched, whining note in the distance.

"Speak up, Mrs. Oakes — I can hardly hear you."

"I can hardly hear you either," said the breathless voice distantly. "There, is that better? I'm shouting now! What time are you leaving in the morning, Mr. Longridge? What's that? Could you talk louder?"

"About seven o'clock. I want to get to Heron Lake before nightfall," he shouted, noting with amusement the scandalized expression of the cat. "But there's no need for you to be here at that time, Mrs. Oakes."

"What's that you said? Seven? Will it be all right if I don't come in until about nine? My niece is coming on the early bus and I'd like to meet her. But I don't like to leave the dogs alone too long. . . ."

"Of course you must meet her," he answered, shouting really loudly now as the humming noise increased. "The dogs will be fine. I'll take them out first thing in the morning, and —"

"Oh, thanks, Mr. Longridge — I'll be there around nine without fail. What's that you said about the animals? (Oh, you pernickety, dratted old line!) Don't you worry about them; Bert and me, we'll see. . . . tell old Bodger . . . bringing marrow bone. Oh, wait till I give that operator a piece of my mi . . ."

But just as Longridge was gathering strength for

a last bellow into the mouthpiece the line went dead. He put the receiver back with relief and looked across the room at the old dog who had climbed stealthily into the armchair and sat lolling back against the cushions, his eyes half closed, awaiting the expected reproof. He addressed him with the proper degree of ferocity, telling him that he was a scoundrelly opportunist, a sybaritic barbarian, a disgrace to his upbringing and his ancestors, "AND" — and he paused in weighty emphasis — "a very . . . *bad* . . . *dog!*"

At these two dread words the terrier laid his ears flat against his skull, slanted his eyes back until they almost disappeared, then drew his lips back over his teeth in an apologetic grin, quivering the end of his disgraceful tail. His parody of sorrow brought its usual reprieve: the man laughed and patted the bony head, then enticed him down with the promise of a run.

So the old dog, who was a natural clown, slithered half off the chair and stood, with his hindquarters resting on the cushions, waving his tail and nudging the cat, who sat like an Egyptian statue, eyes half closed, head erect, then gave a throaty growl and patted at the pink and black bull-terrier nose. Then together they followed the man to the door, where the young dog waited to fall in behind the little procession. Longridge opened the door leading on to the garden, and the two dogs and the cat squeezed past his legs and into the cool night air. He stood under the trellised porch, quietly smoking his pipe, and watched them for a while. Their nightly routine never varied — first the few minutes of separate local investigation, then the indefinable moment when all met again and paused before setting off together through the gap in the hedge at the bottom of the garden and into the fields and woods that lay beyond. He watched until they disappeared into the darkness (the white shape of the bull terrier showing up long after Longridge was unable to distinguish the other two), then knocked his pipe out against the stone step and re-entered the house. It would be half an hour or more before they returned.

Longridge and his brother owned a small cabin by the shores of remote Heron Lake, about two hundred miles away; and twice a year they spent two or three weeks there together, leading the life they loved: spending many hours in companionable silence in their canoe, fishing in spring and hunting in the autumn. Usually he had simply locked up and left, leaving the key with Mrs. Oakes so that she could come in once or twice a week and keep the house warm and aired. However, now he had the animals to consider. He had thought of taking them all to a boarding kennel in the town, but Mrs. Oakes, who loved the assorted trio, had protested vigorously and assented that she herself would look after them "rather than have those poor dumb animals fretting themselves into a state in some kennel, and probably half starved into the bargain." So it had been arranged that she and Bert would look after the three animals. Bert would be working around the garden, anyway, so that they could be outside most of the time and Mrs. Oakes would feed them and keep her eye on them while she was working in the house.

When he had finished packing, Longridge went into the library to draw the curtains, and seeing the telephone he was reminded of Mrs. Oakes. He had forgotten to tell her to order some coffee and other things that he had taken from the store cupboard. He sat down at the desk and drew out a small memo pad.

Dear Mrs. Oakes, he wrote, *Please order some more coffee and replace the canned food I've taken. I will be taking the dogs (and Tao too of course!)* . . . Here he came to the end of the small square of paper, and taking another piece he continued: *. . . out for a run before I leave, and will give them something to eat, so don't let our greedy white friend tell you he is starving! Don't worry yourselves too much over them — I know they will be fine.*

He wrote the last few words with a smile, for the bull terrier had Mrs. Oakes completely in thrall and worked his advantage to the full. He left the pages on the desk under a glass paperweight; then opened the door in answer to a faint scratch. The old dog and the cat bounded in to greet him with their usual affection, bringing the fresh smell of the outdoors with them. The young dog followed more sedately and stood by, watching aloofly, as the other whipped his tail like a lash against the man's legs, while the cat pressed against him purring in a deep rumble; but he wagged his tail briefly and politely when the man patted him.

The cat walked into the library to curl up on the warm hearth. Later when the ashes grew cold he would move to the top of the radiator, and then, sometime in the middle of the night, he would steal upstairs and curl up beside the old dog. It was useless shutting the bedroom door, or any other door of the house for that matter, for the cat could open them all, latches or doorknobs. The only doors that defeated him were those with porcelain handles, for he found it impossible to get a purchase on the shiny surface with his long monkeylike paws.

The young dog padded off to his rug on the floor of the little back kitchen, and the bull terrier started up the steep stairs, and was already curled in his basket in the bedroom when Longridge himself came to bed. He opened one bright, slanted eye when he felt the old blanket being dropped over him, then pushed his head under the cover, awaiting the opportunity he knew would come later.

The man lay awake for a while, thinking about the days ahead and of the animals, for the sheer misery in the young dog's eyes haunted him.

They had come to him, this odd and lovable trio, over eight months ago, from the home of an old and dear college friend. This friend, Jim Hunter, was an English professor in a small university about two hundred and fifty miles away. As the university owned one of the finest reference libraries in the province, Longridge often stayed with him and was, in fact, godfather to the Hunters' nine-year-old daughter, Elizabeth. He had been staying with them when the invitation came from an English university, asking the professor to deliver a series of lectures which would involve a stay in England of nearly nine months, and he had witnessed the tears of his goddaughter and the glum silence of her brother, Peter, when it was decided that their pets would have to be boarded out and the house rented to the reciprocal visiting professor.

Longridge was extremely fond of Elizabeth and Peter, and he could understand their feelings, remembering how much the companionship of a cocker spaniel had meant when he himself was a rather lonely child, and how he had grieved when he was first separated from it. Elizabeth was the self-appointed owner of the cat. She fed and brushed him, took him for walks, and he slept at the foot of her bed. Eleven-year-old Peter had been inseparable from the bull terrier ever since the small white puppy had arrived on Peter's first birthday. In fact, the boy could not remember a day of his life when Bodger had not been part of it. The young dog belonged, in every sense of the word, heart and soul to their father, who had trained him since puppyhood for hunting.

Now they were faced with the realization of separation, and in the appalled silence that followed the decision Longridge watched Elizabeth's face screw up in the prelude to tears. Then he heard a voice, which he recognized with astonishment to be his own, telling everybody not to worry, not to worry at all — he would take care of everything! Were not he and the animals already well known to one another? And had he not plenty of room, and a large garden? . . . Mrs. Oakes? Why, she would just love to have them! Everything would be simply wonderful! Before the family sailed they would bring the dogs and the cat over by car, see for themselves where they would sleep, write out a list of instructions, and he, personally, would love and cherish them until their return.

So one day the Hunter family had driven over and the pets had been left, with many tearful farewells from Elizabeth and last-minute instructions from Peter.

During the first few days Longridge had almost regretted his spontaneous offer: the terrier had languished in his basket, his long arched nose buried in the comfort of his paws, and one despairing, martyred eye haunting his every movement; and the cat had nearly driven him crazy with the incessant goatlike bleating and yowling of a suffering Siamese; the young dog had moped by the door and refused all food. But after a few days, won over perhaps by Mrs. Oakes's sympathetic clucking and tempting morsels of food, they had seemed to resign themselves, and the cat and the old dog had settled in, very comfortably and happily, showing their adopted master a great deal of affection.

It was very apparent, however, how much the

old dog missed children. Longridge at first had won-
dered where he disappeared to some afternoons; he
eventually found out that the terrier went to the
playground of the little rural school, where he was
a great favorite with the children, timing his appearance for recess. Knowing that the road was forbidden to him, because of his poor sight and habit
of walking stolidly in the middle, he had found a
short cut across the intervening fields.

But the young dog was very different. He had
obviously never stopped pining for his own home
and master; although he ate well and his coat was
glossy with health, he never maintained anything
but a dignified, unyielding distance. The man re-
spected him for this, but it worried him that the dog
never seemed to relax, and always appeared to be
listening — longing and waiting for something far
beyond the walls of the house or the fields beyond.
Longridge was glad for the dog's sake that the Hunters would be returning in about three weeks, but
he knew that he would miss his adopted family.
They had amused and entertained him more than he
would have thought possible, over the months, and
he realized tonight that the parting would be a real
wrench. He did not like to think of the too quiet
house that would be his again.

He slept at last, and the dreaming, curious moon
peeped in at the window to throw shafts of pale
light into the rooms and over each of the sleeping
occupants. They woke the cat downstairs, who
stretched and yawned, then leaped without visible

effort onto the window sill, his gleaming eyes, with their slight cast, wide open and enormous, and only the tip of his tail twitching as he sat motionless, staring into the garden. Presently he turned, and with a single graceful bound crossed to the desk; but for once he was careless, and his hind leg knocked the glass paperweight to the floor. He shook the offending leg vigorously, scattering the pages of Longridge's note — sending one page off the desk into the air, where it caught the upward current of hot air from the wall register and sailed across the room to land in the fireplace. Here it slowly curled and browned, until nothing remained of the writing but the almost illegible signature at the bottom.

When the pale fingers of the moon reached over the young dog in the back kitchen he stirred in his uneasy sleep, then sat upright, his ears pricked — listening and listening for the sound that never came: the high, piercing whistle of his master that would have brought him bounding across the world if only his straining ears could hear it.

And lastly the moon peered into the upstairs bed-room, where the man lay sleeping on his side in a great fourposter bed; and curled against his back the elderly, comfort-loving white bull terrier slept in blissful, warm content.

2

THERE WAS a slight mist when John Longridge rose early the following morning, having fought a losing battle for the middle of the bed with his uninvited bedfellow. He shaved and dressed quickly, watching the mist roll back over the fields and the early morning sun break through. It would be a perfect fall day, an Indian summer day, warm and mellow. Downstairs he found the animals waiting patiently by the door for their early morning run. He let them out, then cooked and ate his solitary breakfast. He was out in the driveway, loading up his car when the dogs and cat returned from the fields. He fetched some biscuits for them and they lay by the wall of the house in the early sun, watching him. He threw the last item into the back of the car, thankful that he had already packed the guns and hunting equipment before the Labrador had seen them, then walked over and patted the heads of his audience, one by one.

"Be good," he said. "Mrs. Oakes will be here soon. Good-by, Luath," he said to the Labrador, "I wish I could have taken you with me, but there wouldn't be room in the canoe for three of us." He put his hand under the young dog's soft muzzle. The golden-brown eyes looked steadily into his, and then the dog did an unexpected thing: he lifted his right paw and placed it in the man's hand. Longridge had seen him do this many a time to his own master and he was curiously touched and affected by the trust it conveyed, almost wishing he did not have to leave immediately just after the dog had shown his first responsive gesture.

He looked at his watch and realized he was already late. He had no worries about leaving the animals alone outside, as they had never attempted to stray beyond the large garden and the adjacent fields; and they could return inside the house if they wished, for the kitchen door was the kind that closed slowly on a spring. All that he had to do was shoot the inside bolt while the door was open, and after that it did not close properly and could be pushed open from the outside. They looked contented enough, too — the cat was washing methodically behind his ears — the old dog sat on his haunches, panting after his run, his long pink tongue lolling out of his grinning mouth; and the Labrador lay quietly by his side.

Longridge started the car and waved to them out of the window as he drove slowly down the drive, feeling rather foolish as he did so. "What do I expect them to do in return?" he asked himself with a smile. "Wave back? Or shout 'Good-by'? The trouble is I've lived too long alone with them and I'm becoming far too attached to them."

The car turned around the bend at the end of the long tree-lined drive and the animals heard the sound of the engine receding in the distance. The cat transferred his attention to a hind leg; the old dog stopped panting and lay down; the young dog remained stretched out, only his eyes moving and an occasional twitch of his nose.

Twenty minutes passed by and no move was made; then suddenly the young dog rose, stretched himself, and stood looking intently down the drive. He remained like this for several minutes, while the cat watched closely, one leg still pointing upwards; then slowly the Labrador walked down the driveway and stood at the curve, looking back as though inviting the others to come. The old dog rose too, now, somewhat stiffly, and followed. Together they turned the corner, out of sight.

The cat remained utterly still for a full minute, blue eyes blazing in the dark mask. Then, with a curious hesitating run, he set off in pursuit. The dogs were waiting by the gate when he turned the corner, the old dog peering wistfully back, as though he hoped to see his friend Mrs. Oakes materialize with a juicy bone; but when the Labrador started up the road he followed. The cat still paused by the gate, one paw lifted delicately in the air — undecided, questioning, hesitant; until suddenly, some inner decision reached, he followed the dogs. Presently all three disappeared from sight down the dusty road, trotting briskly and with purpose.

About an hour later Mrs. Oakes walked up the driveway from her cottage, carrying a string bag with her working shoes and apron, and a little parcel of tidbits for the animals. Her placid, gentle face wore a rather disappointed look, because the dogs usually spied her long before she got to the house and would rush to greet her.

"I expect Mr. Longridge left them shut inside the house if he was leaving early," she consoled herself. But when she pushed open the kitchen door and walked inside, everything seemed very silent and still. She stood at the foot of the stairs and called them, but there was no answering patter of running feet, only the steady tick-tock of the old clock in the hallway. She walked through the silent house and out into the front garden and stood there calling with a puzzled frown.

"Oh, well," she spoke her thoughts aloud to the empty, sunny garden, "perhaps they've gone up to the school. . . . It's a funny thing, though," she continued, sitting on a kitchen chair a few minutes later and tying her shoelaces, "that Puss isn't here — he's usually sitting on the window sill at this time of the day. Oh, well, he's probably out hunting — I've never known a cat like that for hunting, doesn't seem natural somehow!"

She washed and put away the few dishes, then

took her cleaning materials into the sitting room. There her eye was caught by a sparkle on the floor by the desk, and she found the glass paperweight, and after that the remaining sheet of the note on the desk. She read it through to where it said: "I will be taking the dogs (and Tao too of course!) . . .", then looked for the remainder. "That's odd," she thought, "now where would he take them? That cat must have knocked the paperweight off last night — the rest of the note must be somewhere in the room."

She searched the room but it was not until she was emptying an ash tray into the fireplace that she noticed the charred curl of paper in the hearth. She bent down and picked it up carefully, for it was obviously very brittle, but even then most of it crumbled away and she was left with a fragment which bore the initials J. R. L.

"Now, isn't that the queerest thing," she said to the fireplace, rubbing vigorously at the black marks on the tile. "He must mean he's taking them all to Heron Lake with him. But why would he suddenly do that, after all the arrangements we made? He never said a word about it on the telephone — but wait a minute, I remember now — he was just going to say something about them when the line went dead; perhaps he was just going to tell me."

While Mrs. Oakes was amazed that Longridge would take the animals on his vacation, it did not occur to her to be astonished that a cat should go along too, for she was aware that the cat loved the car and always went with the dogs when Longridge drove them anywhere or took them farther afield for walks. Like many Siamese cats, he was as obedient and as trained to go on walks as most dogs, and would always return to a whistle.

Mrs. Oakes swept and dusted and talked to the house, locked it and returned home to her cottage. She would have been horrified to the depths of her kindly, well-ordered soul if she had known the truth. Far from sitting sedately in the back of a car traveling north with John Longridge, as she so fondly visualized, the animals were by now many miles away on a deserted country road that ran westward.

They had kept a fairly steady pace for the first hour or so, falling into an order which was not to vary for many miles or days; the Labrador ran always by the left shoulder of the old dog, for the bull terrier was very nearly blind in the left eye, and they jogged along fairly steadily together — the bull terrier with his odd, rolling, sailorlike gait, and the Labrador in a slow lope. Some ten yards behind came the cat, whose attention was frequently distracted, when he would stop for a few minutes and then catch up again. But, in between these halts, he ran swiftly and steadily, his long slim body and tail low to the ground.

When it was obvious that the old dog was flagging, the Labrador turned off the quiet, graveled road and into the shade of a pinewood beside a clear, fast-running creek. The old dog drank deeply, standing up to his chest in the cold water; the cat picked his way delicately to the edge of an over-hanging rock. Afterwards they rested in the deep pine needles under the trees, the terrier panting heavily with his eyes half closed, and the cat busy with his eternal washing. They lay there for nearly an hour, until the sun struck through the branches above them. The young dog rose and stretched, then walked towards the road. The old dog rose too, stiff-legged, his head low. He walked toward the waiting Labrador, limping slightly and wagging his tail at the cat, who suddenly danced into a patch of sun-light, struck at a drifting leaf, then ran straight at the dogs, swerving at the last moment, and as sud-denly sitting down again.

They trotted steadily on, all that afternoon — mostly traveling on the grassy verge at the side of the quiet country road; sometimes in the low over-grown ditch that ran alongside, if the acute hearing of the young dog warned them of an approaching car.

By the time the afternoon sun lay in long, barred shadows across the road, the cat was still traveling in smooth, swift bursts, and the young dog was com-paratively fresh. But the old dog was very weary, and his pace had dropped to a limping walk. They turned off the road into the bush at the side, and walked slowly through a clearing in the trees, push-ing their way through the tangled undergrowth at the far end. They came out upon a small open place where a giant spruce had crashed to the ground and left a hollow where the roots had been, filled now with drifted dry leaves and spruce needles.

The late afternoon sun slanted through the branches overhead, and it looked invitingly snug and secure. The old dog stood for a minute, his heavy head hanging, and his tired body swaying slightly, then lay down on his side in the hollow. The cat, after a good deal of wary observation, made a little hollow among the spruce needles and curled around in it, purring softly. The young dog disappeared into the undergrowth and reappeared presently, his smooth coat dripping water, to lie down a little away apart from the others.

The old dog continued to pant exhaustedly for a long time, one hind leg shaking badly, until his eyes closed at last, the labored breaths came further and further apart, and he was sleeping — still, save for an occasional long shudder.

Later on, when darkness fell, the young dog moved over and stretched out closely at his side and the cat stalked over to lie between his paws; and so, warmed and comforted by their closeness, the old dog slept, momentarily unconscious of his aching, tired body or his hunger.

In the nearby hills a timber wolf howled mournfully; owls called and answered and glided silently by with great outspread wings; and there were faint whispers of movement and small rustling noises around all through the night. Once an eerie wail like a baby's crying woke the old dog and brought him shivering and whining to his feet; but it was only a porcupine, who scrambled noisily and clumsily down a nearby tree trunk and waddled away, still crying softly. When he lay down again the cat was gone from his side — another small night hunter slipping through the unquiet shadows that froze to stillness at his passing.

The young dog slept in fitful, uneasy starts, his muscles twitching, constantly lifting his head and growling softly. Once he sprang to his feet with a full-throated roar which brought a sudden splash in the distance, then silence — and who knows what else unknown, unseen or unheard passed through his mind to disturb him further? Only one thing was clear and certain — that at all costs he was going home, home to his own beloved master. Home lay to the west, his instinct told him; but he could not leave the other two — so somehow he must take them with him, all the way.

3

IN THE COLD HOUR before dawn, the bull
terrier woke, then staggered painfully to his feet.
He was trembling with cold and was extremely
hungry and thirsty. He walked stiffly in the direction of the pool nearby, passing on his way the cat,
who was crouched over something held between
his paws. The terrier heard a crunching sound as the
cat's jaws moved, and, wagging his tail in interest,
moved over to investigate. The cat regarded him
distantly, then stalked away, leaving the carcass;
but to the terrier it was a disappointing mess of
feathers only. He drank long and deeply at the pool
and on his return tried the feathers again, for he was
ravenous; but they stuck in his gullet and he retched
them out. He nibbled at some stalks of grass, then,
delicately, his lips rolled back over his teeth, picked
a few overripe raspberries from a low bush. He had
always liked to eat domestic raspberries this way,
and although the taste was reassuringly familiar, it

did nothing to appease his hunger. He was pleased to see the young dog appear presently; he wagged his tail and licked the other's face, then followed resignedly when a move was made towards the direction of the road. They were followed a few moments later by the cat, who was still licking his lips after his feathery breakfast.

In the gray light of dawn the trio continued down the side of the road until they reached a point where it took a right-angled turn. Here they hesitated before a disused logging trail that led westward from the side of the road, its entrance almost concealed by overhanging branches. The leader lifted his head and appeared almost as though he were searching for the scent of something, some reassurance; and apparently he found it, for he led his companions up the trail between the overhanging trees. The going here was softer; the middle was overgrown with grass and the ruts on either side were full of dead leaves. The close-growing trees which almost met overhead would afford more shade when the sun rose higher. These were all considerations that the old dog needed, for he had been tired today even before he started, and his pace was already considerably slower.

Both dogs were very hungry and watched enviously when the cat caught and killed a chipmunk while they were resting by a stream in the middle of the day. But when the old dog advanced with a hopeful wag of his tail, the cat, growling, retreated into the bushes with his prey. Puzzled and disappointed, the terrier sat listening to the crunching sounds inside the bushes, saliva running from his mouth.

A few minutes later the cat emerged and sat down, daintily cleaning his whiskers. The old dog licked the black Siamese face with his panting tongue and was affectionately patted on the nose in return. Restless with hunger, he wandered up the banks of the creek, investigating every rock and hollow, pushing his hopeful nose through tunnels of withered sedge and into the yielding earth of molehills. Sadly he lay down by an unrewarding blueberry bush, drew his paws down tightly over his blackened face, then licked the dirt off them.

The young dog, too, was hungry; but he would have to be on the verge of starvation before the barriers of deep-rooted Labrador heredity would be broken down. For generations his ancestors had been bred to retrieve without harming, and there was nothing of the hunter in his make-up; as yet, any killing was abhorrent to him. He drank deeply at the stream and urged his companions on.

The trail ran high over the crest of this hilly, wooded country, and the surrounding countryside below was filled with an overwhelming beauty of color; the reds and vermilions of the occasional maples; pale birch, and yellow poplar, and here and there the scarlet clusters of mountain ash berries against a rich dark-green background of spruce and pine and cedar.

Several times they passed log ramps built into the

side of the hill, picking their way across the deep ruts left by the timber sleighs below; and sometimes they passed derelict buildings in rank, overgrown clearings, old stables for the bush horses and living quarters for the men who had worked there a generation ago. The windows were broken and sagging and weeds were growing up between the floorboards, and even one old rusted cookstove had fireweed springing from the firebox. The animals, strangely enough, did not like these evidences of human occupation and skirted them as far as possible, hair raised along their backs.

Late in the afternoon the old dog's pace had slowed down to a stumbling walk, and it seemed as if only sheer determination were keeping him on his feet at all. He was dizzy and swaying, and his heart was pounding. The cat must have sensed this general failing, for he now walked steadily beside the dogs, very close to his tottering old friend, and uttered plaintive worried bleats. Finally, the old dog came to a standstill by a deep rut half-filled with muddy water. He stood there as if he had not even the strength to step around it; his head sagged, and his whole body was trembling. Then, as he tried to lap the water, his legs seemed to crumple under him and he collapsed, half in and half out of the rut. His eyes were closed, and his body moved only to the long, shallow, shuddering breaths that came at widening intervals. Soon he lay completely limp and still. The young dog became frantic now: he whined, as he stretched at the edge of the rut, then nudged and pushed with his nose, doing everything in his power to rouse the huddled, unresponsive body. Again and again he barked, and the cat growled softly and continuously, walking back and forth and rubbing his whole length against the dirty, muddied head. There was no response to their attention. The old dog lay unconscious and remote.

The two animals grew silent, and sat by his side, disturbed and uneasy; until at last they turned and left him, neither looking back — the Labrador disappearing into the bushes where the crack of broken branches marked his progress farther and farther away; the cat stalking a partridge which had appeared at the side of the trail some hundred yards away and was pecking unconcernedly at the sandy dirt. But at the shrill warning of a squirrel, it flew off across the trail with a sudden whirr into the trees, while the cat was still some distance away. Undaunted, still licking his lips in anticipation, the cat continued around a bend in the trail in search of another, and was lost to sight.

The shadows lengthened across the deserted track, and the evening wind sighed down it to sweep a flurry of whispering leaves across the rut, their brown brittleness light as a benison as they drifted across the unheeding white form. The curious squirrel peered in bright-eyed wonder from a nearby tree, clucking softly to itself. A shrew ran halfway across, paused and ran back; and there was a soft sound of wings as a whisky-jack landed and swayed to and fro on a birch branch, tilting his head to one side as he looked down and called to his mate to come and join him. The wind died away — a sudden hush descended.

Suddenly, there was a sound of a heavy body pushing through the underbrush, accompanied by a sharp cracking of branches, and the spell was broken. Chattering shrilly in alarm and excitement, the squirrel ran up the trunk of the tree and the whisky-jacks flew off. Now onto the trail on all fours scampered a half-grown bear cub, round furry ears pricked and small deep-set eyes alight with curiosity in the sharp little face as he beheld the old dog. There was a grunting snuffling sound in the bush behind the cub: his mother was investigating a rotten tree stump. The cub stood for a moment and then hesitantly advanced toward the rut where the terrier lay. He sniffed around, wrinkling his facile nose at the unfamiliar smell, then reached out a long curved black paw and tapped the white head. For a moment the mists of unconsciousness cleared and the old dog opened his eyes, aware of danger. The cub sprang back in alarm and watched from a safe distance. Seeing that there was no further movement, he loped back and cuffed again with his paw, this time harder, and watched for a response. Only enough strength was left in the old dog for a valiant baring of his teeth. He snarled faintly with pain and hatred when his shoulder was raked by the wicked claws of the excited cub, and made an attempt to struggle to his feet. The smell of the drawn blood excited the cub further; he straddled the dog's body and started to play with the long white tail, nibbling at the end like a child with a new toy. But there was no response: all conscious effort drained, the old dog no longer felt any pain or indignity. He lay as though asleep, his eyes veiled and unseeing, his lip still curled in a snarl.

Around the bend in the trail, dragging a large dead partridge by the wing, came the cat. The wing sprang back softly from his mouth as he gazed transfixed at the scene before him. In one split second a terrible transformation took place; his blue eyes glittered hugely and evilly in the black masked face, and every hair on the wheat-colored body stood upright so that he appeared twice his real size; even the chocolate-colored tail puffed up as it switched from side to side. He crouched low to the ground, tensed and ready, and uttered a high, ear-splitting scream; and, as the startled cub turned, the cat sprang.

He landed on the back of the dark furred neck, clinging with his monkeylike hind legs while he raked his claws across the cub's eyes. Again and again he raked with the terrible talons, hissing and spitting in murderous devilry until the cub was screaming in pain and fear, blinded with blood, making ineffectual brushing movements with his paws to dislodge the unseen horror on his back. His screams were answered by a thunderous roar as the huge black she-bear crashed through the bushes and rushed to the cub. She swiped at the clinging cat with a tremendous paw; but the cat was too quick for her and with a hiss of fury leaped to the ground and disappeared behind a tree. The unfortunate cub's head received the full force of the blow and he was sent spinning across the track into the bushes. In a blind, frustrated rage, maddened by the cries of her cub, the mother turned for something on which to vent her fury, and saw the still figure of the old dog. Even as she lumbered snarling towards him the cat distracted her attention with a sudden leap to the side of the track. The bear halted, then reared up to full height for attack, red eyes glinting savagely, neck upstretched and head weaving from side to side in a menacing, snakelike way. The cat uttered another banshee scream and stepped forward with a stiff-legged, sideways movement, his squinting, terrible eyes fixed on his enormous adversary. Something like fear or indecision crept into the bear's eyes as the cat advanced; she shuffled back a step with lowered head. Slow, deliberate, purposeful, the cat came on — again the bear retreated, bewildered by the tactics of this terrible small animal, distraught by her cub's whimpering, slowly falling back before the relentless inch-by-inch advance. Now the cat stopped and crouched low, lashing his tail from side to side — the bear stopped too, shifting her weight uneasily before the spring that must follow, longing to decamp but afraid to turn her back. A sudden crackle of undergrowth turned the huge animal into a statue, rigid with apprehension — and when a great dog sprang out of the bush and stood beside the cat, teeth bared and snarling, every hair on his russet back and ruff erect, she dropped to all fours, turned swiftly and fled towards her cub. There was a last growl of desperate bravado from the bush and a whimpering cry; then the sounds of the bears' escape receded in the distance. Finally all was quiet again; the curious squirrel leaped from his ringside seat and scrambled farther down the trunk of the tree.

The cat shrank back to his normal size. His eyes regained their usual cool, detached look. He shook each paw distastefully in turn, glanced briefly at the limp, muddied bundle by his feet, blood oozing from four deep parallel gashes on the shoulder, then turned and sauntered slowly down the track towards his partridge.

The young dog nosed his friend all over, his lips wrinkling at the rank bear smell, then attempted to stanch the wounds with his rough tongue. He scratched fresh leaves over the bloodstained ones, then barked by the old dog's head; but there was no response, and at last he lay down panting on the grass. His eyes were uneasy and watchful, the hairs still stood upright in a ridge on his back, and from time to time he whined in perplexity. He watched the cat drag a large gray bird almost up to the nose of the unconscious dog, then slowly and deliberately begin to tear at the bird's flesh. He growled softly, but the cat ignored him and continued his tearing and eating. Presently, the enticing smell of raw, warm meat filtered through into the old dog's senses. He opened one eye and gave an appreciative sniff.

The effect was galvanizing: his muddied half-chewed tail stirred and he raised his shoulders, then his forelegs, with a convulsive effort, like an old work horse getting up after a fall.

He was a pitiful sight — the half of his body that had lain in the rut was black and soaking, while the other was streaked and stained with blood. He looked like some grotesque harlequin. He trembled violently and uncontrollably throughout the length of his body, but in the sunken depths of the slanted black-currant eyes there was a faint gleam of interest — which increased as he pushed his nose into the still-warm bundle of soft gray feathers. This time there was no growling rebuff over the prey: instead, the cat sat down a few yards away, studiedly aloof and indifferent, then painstakingly washed down the length of his tail. When the end twitched he pinned it down with a paw.

The old dog ate, crunching the bones ravenously with his blunt teeth. Even as his companions watched him, a miraculous strength slowly seeped back into his body. He dozed for a while, a feather hanging from his mouth, then woke again to finish the last morsel. By nightfall he was able to walk over to the soft grass at the side of the track, where he lay down and blinked happily at his companions, wagging his pitiful tail. The Labrador lay down beside him, and licked the wounded shoulder.

An hour or two later the purring cat joined them, carelessly dropping another succulent morsel by his old friend's nose. This was a deer mouse, a little creature with big eyes and long hind legs like a miniature kangaroo. It was swallowed with a satisfying gulp, and soon the old dog slept.

But the cat purring against his chest and the young dog curled at his back were wakeful and alert most of the remaining night; neither moved from his side.

4

HUNGER was now the ruling instinct in the Labrador and it drove him out to forage in the early dawn. He was desperate enough to try some deer droppings, but spat them out immediately in disgust. While he was drinking from a marsh pool still covered with lily pads, he saw a frog staring at him with goggle eyes from a small stone: measuring the distance carefully, he sprang and caught it in the air as it leaped to safety. It disappeared down his throat in one crunch and he looked around happily for more. But an hour's patient search rewarded him with only two, so he returned to his companions. They had apparently eaten, for there were feathers and fur scattered around and both were licking their lips. But something warned him not to urge his old companion on. The terrier was still utterly exhausted, and in addition had lost a lot of blood from the gashes suffered at the cub's claws the day before. These were stiff and black with blood, and had a tendency to open and bleed slightly with any movement, so all that day he lay peacefully in the warm fall sunshine on the grass sleeping, eating what the cat provided, and wagging his tail whenever one of the others came near.

The young dog spent most of the day still occupied with his ceaseless foraging for food. By evening he was desperate, but his luck turned when a rabbit, already changing to its white winter coat, suddenly started up from the long grass and swerved across his path. Head down, tail flying, the young dog gave chase, swerving and turning in pursuit, but always the rabbit was just out of reach of his hungry jaws. At last, he put all his strength into one violent lunge and felt the warm pulsating prize in his mouth. The generations fell away, and the years of training never to sink teeth into feathers or fur; for a moment the Labrador looked almost wolflike as he tore at the warm flesh and bolted it down in ravenous gulps.

They slept in the same place that night and most of the following day, and the weather mercifully continued warm and sunny. By the third day the old dog seemed almost recovered and the wounds were closed. He had spent most of the day ambling around and sleeping, so that by now he seemed almost frisky and quite eager to walk a little.

So, in the late afternoon, they left the place which had been their home for three days and trotted slowly along the track together again. By the time the moon rose they had traveled several miles, and they had come to the edge of a small lake which the track skirted.

A moose was standing in the water among the lily pads on the far shore, his great antlered head and humped neck silhouetted clearly against the pale moon. He took no notice of the strange animals across the water but thrust his head again and again under the water, raising it high in the air after each immersion, and arching his neck. Two or three water hens swam out from the reeds, a little crested grebe popped up like a jack-in-the-box, in the water beside them, and the spreading ripples of their wake caught the light of the moon. As the three sat, ears pricked, they watched the moose squelch slowly out of the muddy water, shake himself, and turn, cantering up the bank out of sight.

The young dog turned his head suddenly, his nose twitching, for his keen scent had caught a distant whiff of wood smoke, and of something else — something unidentifiable. . . . Seconds later, the old dog caught the scent too, and started to his feet, snuffing and questioning with his nose. His thin whippy tail began to sweep to and fro and a bright gleam appeared in the slanted black-currant eyes. Somewhere, not too far away, were human beings — his world: he could not mistake their message — or refuse their invitation — they were undoubtedly cooking something. He trotted off determinedly in the direction of the tantalizing smell. The young dog followed somewhat reluctantly, and for once the cat passed them both; a little moon-mad perhaps, for he lay in wait to dart and strike, then streaked back into the shadows, only to reappear a second later in an elaborate stalk of their tails. Both dogs ignored him.

The scent on the evening breeze was a fragrant compound of roasting rice, wild-duck stew and wood smoke. When the animals looked down from a hill, tantalized and hungry, they saw six or seven fires in the clearing below — their flames lighting up a semicircle of tents and conical birch-bark shelters against a dark background of trees; flickering over the canoes drawn up on the edge of a wild rice marsh and dying redly in the black waters beyond; and throwing into ruddy relief the high, flat planes of brown Ojibway faces gathered around the centers of warmth and brightness.

The men were a colorful lot in jeans and bright plaid shirts, but the women were dressed in somber colors. Two young boys, the only children there, were going from fire to fire shaking grain in shallow pans and stirring it with paddles as it parched. One man in long soft moccasins stood in a shallow pit trampling husks, half his weight supported on a log frame. Some of the band lay back from the fires, smoking and watching idly, talking softly among themselves; while others still ate, ladling the fragrant contents of a black iron pot onto tin plates. Every now and then one of them would throw a bone back over a shoulder into the bush, and the watching animals gazed hungrily after. A woman stood at the edge of the clearing pouring grain from one bark platter to another, and the loose chaff drifted off on the slight wind like smoke.

The old dog saw nothing of this, but his ears and nose supplied all that he needed to know: he could contain himself no longer and picked his way carefully down the hillside, for his shoulder still pained him. Halfway down he sneezed violently in an eddy of chaff. One of the boys by the fire looked up at the sound, his hand closing on a stone, but the woman nearby spoke sharply, and he waited, watching intently.

The old dog limped out of the shadows and into the ring of firelight, confident, friendly, and sure of his welcome; his tail wagging his whole stern ingratiatingly, ears and lips laid back in his nightmarish grimace. There was a stunned silence — broken by a wail of terror from the smaller boy, who flung himself at his mother — and then a quick excited chatter from the Indians. The old dog was rather offended and uncertain for a moment, but he made hopefully for the nearest boy, who retreated, nervously clutching his stone. But again the woman rebuked her son, and at the sharpness of her tone the old dog stopped, crestfallen. She laid down her basket then, and walked quickly across the ring of firelight, stooping down to look more closely. She spoke some soft words of reassurance, then patted his head gently and smiled at him. The old dog leaned against her and whipped his tail against her black stockings, happy to be in contact with a human being again. She crouched down beside him to run her fingers lightly over his ears and back, and when he licked her face appreciatively, she laughed. At this, the two little boys drew nearer to the dog and the rest of the band gathered around. Soon the old dog was where he most loved to be — the center of attention among some human beings. He made the most of it and played to an appreciative audience; when one of the men tossed him a chunk of meat he sat up painfully on his hindquarters and begged for more, waving one paw in the air. This sent the Indians into paroxysms of laughter, and he had to repeat his performance time and time again, until he was tired and lay down, panting but happy.

The Indian woman stroked him gently in reward, then ladled some of the meat from the pot onto the grass. The old dog limped towards it; but before he ate he looked up in the direction of the hillside where he had left his two companions.

A small stone rebounded from rock to rock, then rolled into the sudden silence that followed.

When a long-legged, blue-eyed cat appeared out of the darkness, paused, then filled the clearing with a strident plaintive voice before walking up to the dog and calmly taking a piece of meat from him, the Indians laughed until they were speechless and hic-cupping. The two little boys rolled on the ground, kicking their heels in an abandonment of mirth, while the cat chewed his meat unmoved; but this was the kind of behavior the bull terrier understood, and he joined in the fun. But he rolled so enthusiastically that the wounds reopened: when he got to his feet again his white coat was stained with blood.

All this time the young dog crouched on the hillside, motionless and watchful, although every driving, urgent nerve in his body fretted and strained at the delay. He watched the cat, well-fed and content, curl himself on the lap of one of the sleepy children by the fire; he heard the faint note of derision in some of the Indians' voices as a little, bent, ancient crone addressed them in earnest and impassioned tones before hobbling over to the dog to examine his shoulder as he lay peacefully before the fire. She threw some cattail roots into a boiling pot of water, soaked some moss in the liquid, and pressed it against the dark gashes. The old dog did not move; only his tail beat slowly. When she had finished, she scooped some more meat onto a piece of birchbark and set it on the grass before the dog; and the silent watcher above licked his lips and sat up, but still he did not move from his place.

But when the fires began to burn low and the Indians made preparations for the night, and still his companions showed no signs of moving, the young dog grew restless. He skirted the camp, moving like a shadow through the trees on the hill behind, until he came out upon the lake's shore a quarter of a mile upwind of the camp. Then he barked sharply and imperatively several times.

The effect was like an alarm bell on the other two. The cat sprang from the arms of the sleepy little Indian boy and ran towards the old dog, who was already on his feet, blinking and peering around rather confusedly. The cat gave a guttural yowl, then deliberately ran ahead, looking back as he paused beyond the range of firelight. The old dog shook himself resignedly and walked slowly after — reluctant to leave the warmth of the fire. The Indians watched impassively and silently and made no move to stop him. Only the woman who had first befriended him called out softly, in the tongue of her people, a farewell to the traveler.

The dog halted at the treeline beside the cat and looked back, but the commanding, summoning bark was heard again, and together the two passed out of sight and into the blackness of the night.

That night they became immortal, had they known or cared, for the ancient woman had recognized the old dog at once by his color and companion: he was the White Dog of the Ojibways, the virtuous White Dog of Omen, whose appearance heralds either disaster or good fortune. The Spirits had sent him, hungry and wounded, to test tribal hospitality; and for benevolent proof to the skeptical they had chosen a cat as his companion — for what *mortal* dog would suffer a cat to rob him of his meat? He had been made welcome, fed and succored: the omen would prove fortunate.

5

THE TRIO journeyed on, the pattern of the next few days being very much the same, free of incident or excitement. Leaving their resting place at daylight, they would jog steadily along by day, their pace determined mainly by the endurance of the old dog. Their favorite sleeping places were hollows under uprooted trees where they were sheltered from the wind, and able to burrow down among the drifted leaves for warmth. At first there were frequent halts and rests, but daily the terrier became stronger; after a week he was lean, but the scars on his shoulders were healing, and his coat was smooth and healthy; in fact, he was in better condition and looked younger and fitter than at the outset of the journey. He had always had a happy disposition, and most of the time looked perfectly content, trotting along through the vast stillness of the bush with stolid, unalterable good humor. He was almost always hungry, but that skillful hunter the cat kept him provided with food which, while scarcely ever satisfying, was adequate by his new standard of living.

It was only the famished young dog who really suffered, for he was not a natural hunter, and wasted a lot of ill-afforded energy in pursuit. He lived mainly on frogs, mice, and the occasional leavings of the other two; sometimes he was lucky enough to frighten some small animal away from its prey, but it was a very inadequate diet for such a large and heavily built dog, and his ribs were beginning to show through the shining coat. He was unable to relax, his constant hunger driving him to forage even when the other two were resting; and he never joined them in their amiable foolery, when sometimes the cat would skitter away in pretended fear from the growling, wagging white dog, often ending in being chased up a tree. Then the Labrador would sit apart, aloof and watchful, nervous and tense. It seemed as though he were never able to forget his ultimate purpose and goal — he was going home; home to his own master, home where he belonged, and nothing else mattered. This lodestone of longing, this certainty, drew him to lead his companions ever westward through wild and unknown country, as unerringly as a carrier pigeon released from an alien loft.

Nomadic life seemed to agree with the cat. He was in fine fettle, sleek and well groomed and as debonair as ever, and had adapted himself so well that at times it appeared as though he were positively enjoying the whole expedition. Sometimes he left the other two for an hour or so at a time, but they had ceased to pay any attention to his absence now, as sooner or later he always reappeared.

They traveled mostly on old abandoned trails, astonishingly plentiful in this virtually uninhabited region; occasionally, they cut straight through the bush. It was fortunate that the Indian summer weather still continued for the short thin coat of the bull terrier could not withstand low temperatures, and although a thicker undercoat was already growing in to compensate it would never be adequate. The cat's coat, too, was thickening, making him appear heavier; the Labrador's needed no reinforcement and was already adapted to all extremes, the flat, thick hairs so close together that they made an almost waterproof surface. The short days were warm and pleasant when the sun was high, but the nights were cold: one night, when there was a sudden sharp frost, the old dog shivered so much that they left the shallow cave of their resting place soon after a bright-ringed moon rose and traveled through the remainder of the night, resting most of the following morning in the warmth of the sun.

The leaves were losing their color rapidly, and many of the trees were nearly bare, but the dogwood and pigeonberry by the sides of the trail still blazed with color, and the Michaelmas daisies and fireweed flourished. Many of the birds of the forest had already migrated; those that were left gathered

into great flocks, filling the air with their restless
chatter as they milled around, the long drawn-out
streamers suddenly wheeling to form a clamorous
cloud, lifting and falling in indecision. They saw
few other animals: the noisy progress of the dogs
warned the shy natural inhabitants long before their
approach; and those that they did meet were too
busy and concerned with their winter preparations
to show much curiosity. The only other bear that
they had encountered was sleek and fat as butter,
complacent and sleepy, his thoughts obviously already running on hibernation, and quite uninter-
ested in strange animals. He was, in fact, sitting on a
log in the sun when the animals saw him; after giving
them a sleepy inspection from his little, deep-set eyes
he yawned and continued the lazy scratching of his
ear. The cat, however, growled angrily to himself
for nearly an hour after this encounter.

The rabbits and weasels had changed to their
white winter coats; a few snow buntings had appeared, and several times they had heard the wild,
free, exultant calling of the wild geese, and had
looked up to see the long black V-shaped skeins
passing overhead on the long journey southwards.
The visitors to the northlands were leaving, and
those who remained were preparing themselves for
the long winter that lay ahead. Soon the whole
tempo, the very pulse of the North, would beat
slower and slower until the snow fell like a soft
coverlet; then, snug and warm beneath in dens and

burrows and hollows, the hibernating animals would sleep, scarcely breathing in their deep unconsciousness, until the spring.

As though aware of these preparations and their meaning, the three adventurers increased their pace as much as was possible within the limits determined by the old dog's strength. On good days they covered as much as fifteen miles.

Since they had left the Indian encampment on the shores of the rice lake they had not seen any human beings, or any sign of human habitation, save once at nightfall when they were nosing around a garbage can outside the darkened cookhouse of a lumber camp deep in the very heart of the bush. Marauding bears had been there recently — their rank, heavy smell still hung on the air, and the cat refused to come nearer, but the old dog, watched by the other, tipped over the heavy can, then tried to pry off the lid with a practiced nose. The can rattled and banged loudly on some rocks and neither dog heard the door opening in the dark building behind. Suddenly a blast of shot ripped through the bottom of the can, blowing the lid off and strewing the contents all over the old dog. Deafened and stunned, he stood for a moment, shaking his head; a second shot clanged against metal and brought him to his senses — he grabbed a bone in passing from the plenty strewn all around, and dashed after the Labrador, running so fast that he outdistanced him. A spray of pellets followed, stinging into their hindquarters so that they leaped simultaneously and redoubled their speed. Soon they were in the shelter of the bush, but it was a long time before they halted for the night. The old dog was so exhausted that he slept until dawn. The pellets had been only momentarily painful, but the incident increased the young dog's wary nervousness.

However, a few days later, despite his care, they had another unexpected encounter. They were drinking at midday from a shallow ford crossing an overgrown track to a worked-out silver mine when a cottontail started up in the bracken across the water. The young dog sprang after, drenching the other two, and they watched the chase — the rabbit's head up, the dog's down, linked in a swerving, leaping rhythm of almost balletlike precision — until it disappeared among the trees.

The terrier shook his coat, spraying the cat again; furious, the cat stalked off.

Alone now, with a brief moment of freedom from the constant daytime urging, the old dog made the most of it. He pottered happily around the lichened rocks and mossy banks, savoring everything with his delicate connoisseur's nose; he flicked the caps of several large fawn mushrooms in some displeasure; a shiny black beetle received his keen attention for a while and he followed it like a bloodhound. Presently he lost interest and sat on it. He yawned, scratched his ear, then rolled lazily on a patch of dried mud. Suddenly he lay quite still, his paws dangling limply, his head turned back on the ground towards the trail: he freed a crumpled ear to listen more intently, then his tail registered his pleased anticipation — someone was walking through the bush towards him. He scrambled to his feet and peered shortsightedly down the trail, his tail curving his hindquarters from side to side in welcome. When an old man carrying a canvas bag appeared, talking quietly to himself, the bull terrier stepped out and awaited him. The old man did not pause: small and bent, he hobbled quickly past, lifting an ancient green felt hat from a crown of white hair as he went, and nodding to the dog with a brief smile of great sweetness. Two little gray-and-white chickadees preceded him, flitting from branch to branch over his head. The old dog fell in contentedly behind. Soon the cat appeared in the distance, running to catch up, his eyes on the chickadees; and far behind the cat again, his mouth framed around the dangling carcass of a rabbit, came the triumphant but deeply suspicious Labrador.

The straggling procession continued along the cool, green tunnel of the trail for half a mile, until the trees thinned out and they came upon a small cabin set back in a clearing within sight of the derelict mine workings. They passed, one after the other, through a small, neatly raked garden, between brown raspberry canes and leafless apple trees, and walked slowly up the few steps to the porch. Here the old man set his bag down, knocked on the green door, paused, then opened it, standing courteously aside to motion his following in before him. The old dog walked in, the cat closely by his shoulder, then the man. The young dog hesitated by the trail's side, his eyes round and distrustful above his burden, then, apparently reassured by the open door, he carefully laid the rabbit down behind a bush, scratching a layer of leaves over it, and, this done, followed the others. They stood in an expectant ring in the middle of the cabin, savoring a delicious, meaty smell.

They watched the old man brush the brim of his hat, hang it on a peg, then hobble over to a small, gleaming wood stove and thrust in another log, washing his hands afterwards in a basin filled from a dipper of water. He lifted the lid off a pot simmering on the stove, and the three watchers licked their lips in anticipation. As he took down four gold-rimmed plates from a dresser, a chipmunk appeared from behind a blue jug on the top shelf. Chattering excitedly he ran up the man's arm to his shoulder, where he sat and scolded the strangers with bright jealous eyes, his little striped body twitching with fury. Two gleaming lamps appeared in the darkness of the cat's face and his tail swished in response, but he restrained himself in deference to his surroundings.

The old man chided the chipmunk lovingly as he set four places at the table, handing it a crust which bulged its cheeks, then ladling four very small portions of stew onto the plates. The little animal's noise fell away to an occasional disgruntled squeak, but he ran from shoulder to shoulder to keep watch on the cat. The old dog edged nearer. Looking very small behind a high-backed chair, the old man stood for a moment with his clear, childlike blue eyes closed and his lips moving, then drew out his chair and sat down. He looked around the table, suddenly irresolute; then his brow cleared, and he rose to draw up the two remaining chairs and a bench. "Do sit down," he said, and at the familiar command the three animals behind him sat obediently.

He ate slowly and fastidiously. Two pairs of hypnotized eyes followed every movement of the fork to his mouth; the third pair remained fixed on the chipmunk. Presently the plate was empty, and the old man smiled around the table; but his smile turned again to bewilderment as he saw the three untouched plates. He considered them long and thoughtfully, then shrugged his shoulders and moved on to the next place. Soon that too came to its confusing end, and, sighing, he moved again. Spellbound, his visitors remained rooted to the floor. Even the old dog, for once, was nonplussed: although he shivered in anticipation and saliva ran from his mouth at the enticing smell, he remained sitting as custom and training decreed.

The old man sat on when the last plate was emptied, lost in his own world, his peaceful stillness diffusing through the little cabin so that the watchers sat graven in their places. A little wind stirred outside, swinging the door wide open on creaking hinges. A grosbeak flew in, to perch on the top, the mellow fall sunshine slanting on his brilliant plumage, and it seemed as though the living silence of the great forest around surged up and in through the open door with the bird's coming, so that the animals stirred uneasily, glancing behind them.

The chipmunk's shrill voice cut through the silence, and its claws scrabbled up the dresser as the cat half sprang — but recollected himself in time and slipped out of the door after the grosbeak instead. In a sudden awakening the old man had started to his feet; he looked around as though wondering where he was, his eyes lighting in surprise on the two dogs by the door. Slow recognition dawned on his face and he smiled down affectionately though his gaze looked through and beyond them. "You must come more often," he said; and to the old dog, who stood wagging his tail at the gentle warmth in the voice, "Remember me most kindly to your dear mother!"

He escorted the dogs to the door; they filed past him, their tails low and still, then walked slowly and with great dignity down the little winding path between the raspberry canes and the apple trees to the overgrown track. Here they waited for a moment while the young dog furtively uncovered his prize, and the cat joined them; then, without looking back, they trotted in close formation out of sight between the trees.

A quarter of a mile farther on the young dog looked carefully around before dropping his rabbit. He nudged it with his nose several times, then turned it over. A moment later its red-stained fur lay scattered and both dogs were eating ravenously, growling amicably as they crunched. The cat sat, flexing his claws as he watched. After a while he rose on his hind legs and stretched his forepaws to their full extent against a tree, then methodically sharpened their claws on the bark. His head turned sharply and he paused, still standing, at a rustle in the long dead grass: a split second later he pounced in a bounding arc; a paw flashed out, pinned down and held, his head bent down; and a small squeaking broke off abruptly. Before the dogs were even aware that he had gone he was back again by his tree, cleaning his whiskers with soft rounded paws.

The following day the travelers came down from the hills to find themselves on the banks of a river running north and south. It was about a hundred feet across to the far bank, and although shallow enough in the ordinary way, was far too deep for the animals to cross without swimming. The young dog led the way downstream for some distance looking for a means of crossing, as it was obvious that his companions would not even wet their feet if they could possibly help it, both sharing a great dislike of water. Once or twice he plunged in and swam around, looking back at the other two, obviously trying to entice them by showing them how easy it was, but they remained sitting close together on the bank, united in misery, and he was forced to continue trotting downstream, becoming increasingly worried as he went, aware that it was the wrong direction.

It was lonely, uninhabited country, so that there were no bridges, and the river if anything became wider as they trotted along the banks. After three or four miles the young dog could endure the frustration no longer; he plunged into the water and swam rapidly and strongly across to the far side, his tail streaming out behind like an otter's. He loved the water, and was as much at home in it as the other two hated and feared it. He stood on the far bank, barking encouragingly, but the old dog whined in such distress, the cat yowling in chorus, that he swam across again, paddling around in the shallows near the bank. The old dog walked gingerly into the shallow water, shivering and miserable, turning his head away. Once more the Labrador swam the river, climbed out on the far side, shook himself, and barked. There was no mistaking the command. The old dog took another reluctant step forward, whining piteously, his expressive tail tucked under. The barking continued; again the terrier advanced; again the Labrador swam across to encourage him. Three times he swam across, and the third time the old dog waded in up to his chest and started swimming. He was not a very good swimmer; he swam in jerky rapid movements, his head held high out of the water, his little black eyes rolling fearfully; but he was a bull terrier, a "white cavalier," and he kept on, following the wake of the other, until at last he climbed out on the far side. His transports of joy on reaching dry land were like those of a shipwrecked mariner after six weeks at sea on a raft: he rushed in circles, he rolled on his back, he ran along with alternate shoulders low in the long grass to dry himself, until finally he joined the Labrador on the bank to bark encouragingly at the cat.

The poor cat now showed the first signs of fear since leaving on his journey; he was alone, and the only way to rejoin his friends lay in swimming across the terrible stretch of water. He ran up and down the bank, all the time keeping up his unearthly Siamese wailing. The young dog went through the same tiring performance that he had used before, swimming to and fro, trying to entice him into the water; but the cat was beside himself with terror and it was a long long time before he finally made up his mind. When he did it was with a sudden blind desperate rush at the water, completely un-catlike. His expression of horror and distaste was almost comical as he started swimming towards the young dog who waited for him a few yards out. He proved to be a surprisingly good swimmer, and was making steady progress across, the dog swimming alongside, when tragedy struck.

Many years before a colony of beavers had dammed a small creek which had tumbled into the river about two miles upstream. Since the beavers had left, the dam had been crumbling and loosening gradually, until it had become just a question of time before it would give way altogether, and drain the flooded land behind. Now, by a twist of fate, a rotting log gave way and a large section bulged forward under the added strain. Almost as the two animals reached midstream the dam broke alto-gether. The pent-up force of the unleashed creek leaped through the gap in an ever-widening torrent, carrying everything before it and surging into the river, where it became a swift mountainous wave — carrying small trees, torn-away branches, pieces of riverbank and beaver dam before it on the crest. The young dog saw the onrushing wave several moments before it reached them, and frantically tried to swim into a position upstream of the cat, instinctively try-ing to protect him; but he was too late, and the great curling, crested wave surged over, submerging them in a whirling chaos of debris. The end of a log struck the cat full on the head; he was swept under and over and over until his body was finally caught on a half-submerged piece of the old dam, and was car-ried along on the impetus of the wave as it tore down the river bed.

The old dog, barking wildly in anxiety — for he had sensed the disaster although he could not see it — waded chest-deep into the churning water, but its force knocked him back again, breathless and choking; he was forced to retreat.

The other dog, strong swimmer though he was, made his way to the bank only with the greatest difficulty. Even then he was carried almost half a mile downstream before his feet were on firm ground. Immediately he set off, down the riverside, in pursuit.

Several times he saw the little figure of the cat,

half under water, surging ahead on the swift white crest; but he was never near enough, except at one point where the partially submerged piece of beaver dam caught on an overhanging branch. He plunged in immediately; but just as he was nearly within reach it tore free and once more went whirling down the river until it was lost to sight.

Gradually the dog fell farther and farther behind. At last he was brought to a complete halt when the river entered a rocky gorge with no foothold on either side. He was forced to climb inland, and by the time he rejoined the river bank on the far side of the gorge there was no sign of the cat.

It was nearly dark when he returned to find the terrier, who was walking wearily towards him along the riverbank; the Labrador was exhausted, limping, and utterly spent and miserable — so much so that he barely returned the greeting of the bewildered and lonely old dog but dropped to the ground, his flanks heaving, and lay there until thirst drove him to the water's edge.

They spent that night where they were, by the bank of the river, peaceful at last after the violence of the afternoon. They lay curled closely together for comfort and warmth, and when a thin, cold rain fell as the wind rose they moved under the spreading branches of an old spruce for shelter.

In the middle of the night the old dog sat up, trembling all over with cold. He threw his head back and howled his requiem of grief and loneliness to the heavy, weeping sky; until at last the young dog rose wearily and led him away from the river, long before dawn broke, and over the hills to the west.

6

MANY MILES downstream on the side to which the dogs had crossed, a small cabin stood near the bank of the river, surrounded by three or four acres of cleared land, its solid, uncompromising appearance lightened only by the scarlet geraniums at the window sills and a bright blue door. A log barn stood back from it, and a steam-bath house at the side nearer the river. The patch of vegetable garden, the young orchard and the neatly fenced fields, each with their piles of cleared boulders and stumps, were small orderly miracles of victory won from the dark encroaching forest that surrounded them.

Reino Nurmi and his wife lived here, as sturdy and uncompromising as the cabin they had built with their own hand-hewn logs, their lives as frugal and orderly as the fields they had wrested from the wilderness. The had tamed the bush, and in return it yielded them their food and their scant living from trap lines and a wood lot, but the struggle to keep it in subjection was endless. They had retained their Finnish identity complete when they left their homeland, exchanging only one country's set of solitudes and vast lonely forests for another's, and as yet their only real contact with the new world that lay beyond their property line was through their ten-year-old daughter Helvi, who knew no other homeland. Helvi walked the lonely miles to the waiting school bus each day, and through her they strengthened their roots in the security of the New World, and were content meanwhile with horizons limited by their labor.

On the Sunday afternoon that the beaver dam broke, a day of some relaxation, Helvi was down by the river, skipping flat stones across the water, and wishing that she had a companion; for she found it difficult to be entirely fair in a competition always held against herself. The riverbank was steep and high here, so she was quite safe when a rushing torrent of water, heralded by a great curling wave, swept past. She stood watching it, fascinated by the spectacle, thinking that she must go and tell her father, when her eye was caught by a piece of debris that had been whirling around in a back eddy and was now caught on some boulders at the edge of the bank. She could see what looked like a small, limp body on the surface. She ran along by the boiling water to investigate, scrambling down the bank, to stand looking pityingly at the wet, bedraggled body, wondering what it was, for she had never seen anything like it before. She dragged the mass of twigs and branches further up on land, then ran to call her mother.

Mrs. Nurmi was out in the yard by an old wood stove which she still used for boiling the vegetable dyes for her weaving, or peelings and scraps for the hens. She followed Helvi, calling out to her husband to come and see this strange animal washed up by an unfamiliar, swift-surging river.

He came, with his unhurried countryman's walk and quiet thoughtful face, and joined the others to look down in silence at the small limp body, the darkly plastered fur betraying its slightness, the frail skull bones and thin crooked tail mercilessly exposed. Suddenly he bent down and laid his hand lightly on it for a moment, then pulled back the skin above and below one eye and looked more closely. He turned and saw Helvi's anxious, questioning face close to his own, and beyond that her mother's. "Is a drowned *cat* worth trying to save?" he asked them, and when her mother nodded, before Helvi's pleading eyes, he said no more, but scooped the soaking bundle up and walked back to the cabin, telling Helvi to run ahead and bring some dry sacks.

He laid the cat down in a sunny patch by the wood stove and rubbed it vigorously with sacking, turning the body from side to side until the fur stood out in every direction and it looked like some disheveled old scarf. Then, as he wrapped the sacking firmly around and her mother pried the clenched teeth open, Helvi poured a little warm milk and precious brandy down the pale cold throat.

She watched as a spasm ran through the body, followed by a faint cough, then held her breath in sympathy as the cat retched and choked convulsively, a thin dribble of milk appearing at the side of its mouth. Reino laid the straining body over his knee and pressed gently over the ribcage. The cat choked and struggled for breath, until at last a sudden gush of water streamed out, and it lay relaxed. Reino gave a slow smile of satisfaction and handed the bundle of sacking to Helvi, telling her to keep it warm and quiet for a while — if she was sure that she still wanted a cat.

She felt the oven, still warm though the fire had long died out, then placed the cat on a tray inside, leaving the door open. When her mother went into the cabin to prepare supper and Reino left to milk the cow, Helvi sat cross-legged on the ground by the stove, anxiously chewing the end of one fair braid, watching and waiting. Every now and then she would put her hand into the oven to touch the cat, to loosen the sacking or to stroke the soft fur, which was beginning to pulsate with life under her fingers.

After half an hour she was rewarded: the cat opened his eyes. She leaned over and looked closely into them — their blackness now contracted, slowly, to pinpoints, and a pair of astonishingly vivid blue eyes looked up instead. Presently, under her gentle stroking, she felt a throaty vibration, then heard a rusty, feeble purring. Wildly excited, she called to her parents.

Within another half-hour the little Finnish girl held in her lap a sleek, purring, Siamese cat, who had already finished two saucers of milk (which normally he detested, drinking only water), and who had groomed himself from head to foot. By the time the Nurmi family were eating their supper around the scrubbed pine table, he had finished a bowl of chopped meat, and was weaving his way around the table legs, begging in his plaintive, odd voice for more food, his eyes crossed intently, his kinked tail held straight in the air like a banner. Helvi was fascinated by him, and by his gentleness when she picked him up.

That night the Nurmis were having fresh pickerel, cooked in the old-country way with the head still on and surrounded by potatoes. Helvi ladled the head with some broth and potatoes into a saucer and put it on the floor. Soon the fishhead had disappeared to the accompaniment of pleased rumbling growls. The potatoes followed; then, holding down the plate with his paw, the cat polished it clean. Satisfied at last, he stretched superbly, his front paws extended so that he looked like a heraldic lion, then jumped onto Helvi's lap, curled himself around and purred loudly.

The parents' acceptance was completed by his action, though there had never before been a time or place in the economy of their lives for an animal which did not earn its keep, or lived anywhere else except the barn or kennel. For the first time in her life Helvi had a pet.

Helvi carried the cat up to bed with her, and he draped himself with familiar ease over her shoulder as she climbed the steep ladder stairs leading up to her little room in the eaves. She tucked him tenderly into an old wooden cradle, and he lay in sleepy contentment, his dark face incongruous against a doll's pillow.

Late in the night she woke to a loud purring in her ear, and felt him treading a circle at her back. The wind blew a gust of cold rain across her face and she leaned over to shut the window, hearing far away, so faint that it died in the second of wind-borne sound, the thin, high keening of a wolf. She shivered as she lay down, then drew the new comforting warmth of the cat closely to her.

When Helvi left in the morning for the long walk and ride to the distant school the cat lay curled on the window sill among the geraniums. He had eaten a large plate of oatmeal, and his coat shone in the sun as he licked it sleepily, his eyes following Mrs. Nurmi as she moved about the cabin. But when she went outside with a basket of washing she looked back to see him standing on his hind legs peering after, his soundless mouth opening and shutting behind the window. She hurried back, fearful of her geraniums, and opened the door — at which he was already scratching — half expecting him to run. Instead he followed her to the washing line and sat by the basket, purring. He followed her back and forth between the cabin and the wood stove, the henhouse and the stable. When she shut him out once by mistake he wailed pitifully.

This was the pattern of his behavior all day — he shadowed the Nurmis as they went about their chores, appearing silently on some point of vantage — the seat of the harrow, a sack of potatoes, the manger or the well platform — his eyes on them constantly. Mrs. Nurmi was touched by his apparent need for companionship: that his behavior was unlike that of any other cat she attributed to his foreign appearance. But her husband was not so easily deceived — he had noticed the unusual intensity in the blue eyes. When a passing raven mocked the cat's voice and he did not look up, then later sat unheeding in the stable to a quick rustle in the straw behind, Reino knew then that the cat was deaf.

Carrying her schoolbooks and lunch pail, Helvi ran most of the way home across the fields and picked up the cat as well when he came to meet her. He clung to her shoulder, balancing easily, while she performed the routine evening chores that awaited her. Undeterred by his weight she fed the hens, gathered eggs, fetched water, then sat at the table stringing dried mushrooms. When she put him down before supper she saw that her father was right — the pointed ears did not respond to any sound, though she noticed that he started and turned his head at the vibration if she clapped her hands or dropped even a small pebble on the bare floor.

She had brought home two books from the traveling library, and after the supper dishes had been cleared away her parents sat by the stove in the short interval before bed while she read aloud to them, translating as she went. They sat, in their moment of rare relaxation, with the cat stretched out on his back at their feet, and the child's soft voice, flowing through the dark austerity of the cabin, carried them beyond the circle of light from the oil lamp to the warmth and brightness of strange lands. . . .

They heard of seafaring Siamese cats who worked their passages the world over, their small hammocks made and slung by their human messmates, who held them second to none as ship's cats; and of the great proud Siamese Ratting Corps who patrolled the dockyards of Le Havre with unceasing vigilance; they saw, with eyes withdrawn and dreaming, the palace watch-cats of long-ago Siam, walking delicately on long simian legs around the fountained courtyards, their softly padding feet polishing the mosaics to a lustred path of centuries. And at last they learned how these nobly-born Siamese acquired the kink at the end of their tails and bequeathed it to all their descendants.

And as they listened, they looked down in wonder, for there on the rag rug lay one of these, stretched out flat on his royal back, his illustrious tail twitching idly, and his jeweled eyes on their daughter's hand as she turned the pages that spoke of his ancestors — the guardian cats of the Siamese princesses. Each princess, when she came down to bathe in the palace lake, would slip her rings for safekeeping on the tail of her attendant cat. So zealous in their charge were these proud cats that they bent the last joint sideways for safer custody, and in time the faithful tails became crooked forever, and their childrens' and their childrens' children. . . .

One after another the Nurmis passed their hands admiringly down the tail before them to feel the truth in its bent bony tip; then Helvi gave him a bowl of milk, which he drank with regal condescension before she carried him up the ladder to bed.

That night, and for one more, the cat lay curled peacefully in Helvi's arms, and in the daytime during her absence he followed her parents everywhere. He trailed through the bush after her mother as she searched for late mushrooms, then sat on the cabin steps and patted the dropped corn kernels as she shucked a stack of cobs. He followed Reino and his work horse across the fields to the wood lot and perched on a newly felled pungent stump, his head following their every movement, and he curled by the door of the stable and watched the man mending harness and oiling traps. And in the late afternoons when Helvi returned he was there waiting for her, a rare and beautiful enigma in the certain routine of the day. He was one of them.

But on the fourth night he was restless, shaking his head and pawing his ears, his voice distressed at her back. At last he lay down, purring loudly, and pushed his head into her hand — the fur below his ears was soaking. She saw their sharp black triangles outlined against the little square of window and watched them flicker and quiver in response to every small night sound. Glad for him in his new-found hearing, she fell asleep.

When she woke, later in the night, aware of a lost warmth, she saw him crouched at the open window, looking out over the pale fields and the tall, dark trees below. His long sinuous tail thrashed to and fro as he measured the distance to the ground. Even as her hand moved out impulsively towards him he sprang, landing with a soft thud.

She looked down and saw his head turn for the first time to her voice, his eyes like glowing rubies as they caught the moonlight, then turn away — and with sudden desolate knowledge she knew that he had no further need of her. Through a blur of tears, she watched him go, stealing like a wraith in the night towards the river that had brought him. Soon the low swiftly running form was lost among the shadows.

7

THE TWO DOGS were in very low spirits when they continued their journey without the cat. The old dog in particular moped badly, for the cat had been his constant close companion for many years — ever since the day when a small, furiously hissing kitten, with comically long black-stockinged legs and a nearly white body, had joined the Hunter family. This apparition had refused to give one inch of ground to the furious and jealous bull terrier, who was an avowed cat hater, and the terror of the nearby feline population; instead it had advanced, with every intention of giving battle evident in the tiny body. The dog, for the first time and last time in his life, capitulated. That day a bond had been formed between them, and thereafter they had been inseparable. The kitten, surprisingly enough, had no love for cats either, so they formed a wickedly humorous partnership that waged unceasing war against them. When they sallied forth together the neighborhood emptied suddenly of not only cats but of dogs as well. They had mellowed with the years, however, and were now more tolerant, exacting only the dutiful homage they felt to be their due as conquerors. They had opened their ranks only to the gentle young dog when he arrived years later; but, fond as they were of him, the affection they bore for one another was something quite apart.

Now the dogs were thrown completely on their own resources. The Labrador did his best and tried to initiate the other into the art of frog and field mouse hunting, but the terrier's eyesight was too poor for him to have much success. But they were luckier than usual: once they surprised a large fisher in the very act of dispatching a porcupine. The shy fisher disappeared in one swift fluid movement at their approach, leaving the slain, outstretched porcupine, and the dogs enjoyed a feast that day such as they had never known before, the flesh being sweet and tender.

Another time the young dog caught a bittern, who had stood like a frozen statue on the edge of a lake, his long neck topped by the slim head flowing into a line down to the elongated body, and nothing moving but an apprehensive, blinking eye. He took off as the dog sprang, but his awkward clumsy flight, the long legs trailing, was not fast enough. The flesh was stringy and fishy, but it was all gobbled down voraciously, nothing remaining but the beak and feet.

One day they skirted a small farm, where, wary though he was of human beings, the young dog was hungry enough to cross an open field within sight of the farm and snatch one of a flock of chickens feeding there. They were still crouched over the mess of blood and scattered feathers, when they heard an angry shout, and saw the figure of a man at the far corner of the field, and a black collie running ahead, snarling as it came towards them.

The young dog braced himself for the inevitable attack; a few yards away the collie crouched low, lips drawn back, then sprang for the vulnerable throat before him. The young dog was a hopeless fighter, lacking both the instinct and the build; for, heavy and strong though he was, his mouth had been bred to carry game birds, and the jaw structure, with its soft protective lips, was a disadvantage. His only hope for survival against the razor-like slashing of the other dog's teeth lay in the thick protective folds of skin around his throat.

All too soon it was obvious that he was fast losing ground, and the effects of his inadequate diet were beginning to show in his endurance. He was on his back with the collie on top, ready to give the final slash, when the old dog took over. Up to now he had merely been an interested spectator, taking a keen interest from a professional point of view, for a good fight is meat and drink to a bull terrier. Now a look of pure, unholy joy appeared in the black-currant eyes, and he tensed his stocky, close-knit body, timing his spring with a mastery born of long

practice. A white, compact bundle of fighting art
shot like a steel projectile to the collie's throat. The
impact knocked the black dog over as though he
were a feather; the ecstatic bull terrier tightened his
grip on the sinewy throat under him and began to
shake his head; out of the corner of his eye he
noticed that the Labrador was on his feet again.
But the terrier's teeth were blunt nowadays, and
with a tremendous effort the collie threw him off.
The old dog's feet had barely touched the ground
before he sprang again for that terrible throat grip,
springing as if the years had dropped away and
he were back in his fighting prime. Once more he
brought the collie down, this time taking a firmer
grip on the throat, shaking his powerful head until
the dog below him was choking and strangling. The
collie made a desperate, convulsive effort and rolled
over, the silent white leech still hanging from his
throat. He struggled to his feet: the terrier released
his hold and walked away, his back turned arrogant-
ly but his eyes slewed slyly in his flat head so that he
looked almost reptilian. The collie stood shakily,
blood dripping from his throat, awaiting the protection of his master. Normally he was a courageous
dog, but he had never before encountered anything
like these vicious, silent onslaughts.

The Labrador would have called it a day and
left now, but the terrier was enjoying himself and
still eyed the collie speculatively. Then his peculiar
blend of bull terrier humor got the better of him,

and he used an old fighting trick of his breed, which normally he kept, so to speak, up his sleeve, for those occasions when he intended not a killing, but merely punishment. He started to circle, faster and faster, almost as though he were chasing his own tail, and then, like a whirling dervish, he approached the bewildered collie and spun against him, knocking him several feet with the force of the impact, and following up his advantage with another crash at the end of each turn. Terrified at this unprecedented method of attack, bruised, bitter and aching, the enemy dog seized a split second between turns and fled, his tail tucked well between his legs, towards his master — who received him with a cuff on his already reeling head.

The farmer stared incredulously at the two culprits, who were now making off across the field to the cover of the bush, the young dog with a torn and bloodied ear, and several deep bites on his forelegs, but the happy old warrior jaunty and unscathed. When he saw the mass of feathers he flung his stick in sudden rage at the retreating white form, but so many sticks had been thrown after so many fights in the course of his long life that the bull terrier dodged it instinctively without even turning his head and continued at a leisurely trot, swinging his rounded stern with gay insolence as he went.

This battle did much to restore the morale of the old dog. That evening he even caught a field mouse for his supper, tossing it in the air with a professional flip which would have done credit to his ancestor who had killed sixty rats in as many minutes a hundred years ago.

Despite the stiffness and soreness from his wounds the young dog seemed happier too; perhaps because the west wind that blew that night brought a hint of remembered things, and stirred some deep awareness that every day, every hour brought them nearer to their destination; perhaps it was that the country they were crossing now was less rugged, less remote, and becoming more like the country in which he had been raised; perhaps it was just because his companion was so infectiously pleased with himself; but whatever it was, he seemed more at ease and less strained than he had been since the outset of the journey.

They slept that night in a dry shallow cave amongst the outcroppings of an abandoned molybdenum mine on the crest of a hill. Outside the cave was a large, sloping slab of exposed rock littered with discarded garter-snake skins, so light and dry yet supple that all night long they swayed and whispered to every small breath of wind as though repossessed.

The first pale streaks of dawn were barely showing across the sky when the young dog sat up alertly, hearing the shuffling approach of some animal through the dead leaves and twigs. He sat quivering, every nerve tense, recognizing the smell, and presently past the opening of the cave waddled a large porcupine, returning peacefully home from a night's foraging. Remembering the delectable meal the fisher had inadvertently provided for him, the young dog determined to repeat it. He sprang at the porcupine, intending first to overturn then kill it as he had seen the other animal do, but unfortunately he had not seen the patient preparatory work that the experienced fisher had put in before the kill — the relentless, cunning teasing, resulting in the harmless embedding of most of the quills into a fallen tree; then the quick, skillful flip at the base of the shoulder while the partially unarmed animal was still protecting its tender nose and throat under the tree. The porcupine turned at the instant of his spring, aware of the danger, and with incredible swiftness for such a clumsy-looking animal, spun round, whipping its terrible tail in the dog's face. The dog yelped and leaped back with the unexpected shock of pain, and the porcupine ambled away, looking almost outraged.

The Labrador was fortunate in that the tail had struck a sidewise, glancing blow, so that the quills had pierced only one side of his cheek, missing the eye by a fraction; but these quills were about two-and-a-half inches long, barbed at the piercing end, and were firmly and painfully embedded.

Try as he might the dog could do nothing to remove the pliant quills; he only succeeded in pushing them farther in. He tore at them with his paws; he scratched at the sites until they bled; he rubbed his head and cheek along the ground and against the trunk of a tree. But the cruel, stinging barbs dug in farther, and their stinging torture spread through his face and jaws. Eventually he abandoned the attempt to free them, and they journeyed on. But every time they paused the Labrador would shake his head, or scratch frantically with his hind leg, seeking release from the pain.

8

THE CAT by himself was a swift and efficient traveler. He had no difficulty at all in picking up the trail of the dogs from the point where they had turned off in a westward direction from the river, and the only thing that held him back was rain, which he detested. He would huddle miserably under shelter during a shower, his ears laid flat, his eyes baleful and more crossed than ever, waiting until the last drop had fallen before venturing out again. Then he would pick his way with extreme distaste through the wet grass and undergrowth, taking a long time, and stopping often to shake his paws.

He left no trace of his progress; branches parted slightly here and there, sometimes there was a momentary rustling of dried leaves, but never a twig cracked, and not a stone was dislodged from under his soft, sure feet. Without his noisier companions he saw everything and was seen by none, many an animal remaining unaware of the cold, silent scrutiny in the undergrowth, or from up a tree. He came within touching distance of the soft-eyed deer drinking at the lake's edge at dawn; he watched the sharp, inquisitive nose and bright eyes of a fox peer from the bushes; he saw the sinuous twisting bodies and mean vicious faces of mink and marten; once he looked up and saw the otterlike head of a fisher high above him, framed in the leafless branches of a birch, and watched the beautiful tail stream out behind when the animal leaped a clear fifteen feet through the air into the swaying green obscurity of a pine; and he watched with disdain the lean gray timber wolf loping quietly along the trail beneath him as he rested on the limb of a tree above. Those that he encountered face to face would not meet his eyes and turned away. Only the beaver went about their business and paid him no heed.

Age-old instinct told him to leave no trace of his passing; the remains of the prey he killed with such efficient dispatch were all dug into the ground and covered over; any excreta were taken care of in the same fashion, fresh earth being carefully scraped over. When he slept, which was seldom, it was a quick "cat nap" high in the thick branches of evergreens. He was infinitely cunning and resourceful always, and above all he feared nothing.

On the second morning of his travels he came down at dawn to drink at the edge of a reed-fringed lake; he passed within a hundred feet of a rough, concealing structure of reeds and branches on the lake shore, in which crouched two men, guns across their knees, and a Chesapeake dog. A fleet of decoy ducks bobbed realistically up and down in the water in front of them. The dog stirred uneasily, turning his head and whining softly when the cat passed by, silent and unseen, but one of the men bade him be quiet, and he lay down, ears pricked and eyes alert.

The cat stayed staring at him from behind some bulrushes for a while, then raised his tail so that it alone was in sight and twitched the end, enjoying the dog's silent frustration. He turned and stole silently down to the lake shore, where presently his long slim body, crouched on a rock, was seen in the binoculars of one of the men.

"Here, kitty, kitty!" called an uncertain voice, after a moment's silence. Then "Puss, puss . . . here, puss!" it tried, in gruff embarrassment — ignored by the cat, who curled his pink tongue down to the water and drank slowly and deliberately. Two voices called now, with an undertone of laughing disbelief. He raised his head and looked directly at the two figures standing up, black against the sky.

He heard their excited argument, and then, an intentional poseur, he shook each paw daintily in turn, stepped delicately down from the rocks, and vanished from the men's sight. Behind him he heard a burst of incredulous laughter, and continued on his way, well satisfied.

The cat went on through the early morning mists, still following the trail of the dogs; and here it could not have been very old, for he found a partly chewed rabbit-skin, and several other clues, near some rocks where they had evidently passed a night, and the scent was still quite sharp to his acute sense. They had cut across country at one point through several miles of deep spruce and cedar swamp, so that the going was, alternately, soft and dry and strewn with needles, then damp and spongy. It was a gloomy place, and the cat appeared uneasy, frequently glancing behind him as if he thought he were being followed. Several times he climbed a tree and crouched on a branch, watching and waiting. But whatever it was he scented or imagined showed equal cunning, and never appeared.

But the cat remained wary and suspicious, and felt with every nerve in his body that something was following — something evil. He increased his pace, then saw with relief that the area of deep, gloomy bush was coming to an end: far ahead of him he could see patches of blue sky which meant more open country. An old fallen tree lay ahead of him on the deer trail he was following. He leaped onto the trunk to cross it, pausing for a brief second, then every hair on his back rose erect, for in that moment he heard quite distinctly and felt rather than saw the presence of the following animal — and it was not very far behind him. Without further delay the cat leaped for the trunk of a birch tree, and clinging with his claws looked back along the path. Into view, moving with a velvet tread that equaled his own, came what appeared to be a large cat. But it was as different from the ordinary domestic cat as the Siamese himself was different.

This one was almost twice as large, chunky and heavy, with a short bobtail and thick furry legs. The coat was a soft gray, overlaid with a few darker spots. The head differed only from an ordinary cat in that it was framed in a ruff of hair, and the ears rose into tufted points. It was a wild, cruel face that the Siamese saw, and he recognized instinctively a wanton killer — and one that could easily outclass him in strength, ferocity and speed. He scrambled as far up the young birch as he could go, and clung there, the slender trunk swaying under his weight. The lynx stopped in the center of the trail, one heavy paw lifted, gazing up with gleaming malicious eyes; the Siamese flattened his ears and spat venomously, then looked quickly around, measuring his distance for escape. With a light bound the lynx landed on top of the fallen tree trunk, and for another endless moment the two pairs of eyes tried to outstare one another, the Siamese making a low eerie hissing noise, lashing his tail from side to side. The lynx leaped for the birch, straddling it easily with powerful limbs; then, digging in the long claws, he started up the trunk towards the cat, who retreated as far as was possible, and waited, swaying perilously now.

As the heavy weight came nearer, the tree bent right over, and it was all that the cat could do to hold on. The lynx reached a paw out to its full length and raked at the cat, tearing a strip of the bark away. The cat struck back, but the tree was waving wildly, and he lost his grip with the movement, and fell. The tree was so far bent over that he had not too far to fall, but even in that short time he twisted in the air and landed on his feet, only to hear a heavier thud a few yards away; the tree, whipping back, had dislodged the lynx almost at the same time, but the heavier animal had fallen with more impetus and less agility; for a split second it remained where it was, slightly winded. The cat took his advantage of that second and was off like a streak, running for his life up a narrow deer trail.

Almost immediately he heard the other animal close behind. It was useless to turn and fight; this was no stupid bear who could be intimidated, but a creature as remorseless and cunning as the cat himself could be, to other smaller animals. Even as he ran he must have known that flight was hopeless too; for he leaped with desperation up the trunk of another tree; but they were all saplings and there was little length of trunk for him to climb. This time the enemy was more cunning: it followed only halfway up, then deliberately swayed the pliant young tree from side to side, determined to shake the cat off. The situation was desperate and the cat knew it. He waited until he was on the lowest arc of the swing, then, gathering up his muscles under him until he was like a coiled spring, he leaped for the ground. The lynx was almost as quick, but it missed by a hair's breadth when the cat swerved violently, then doubled on his tracks and shot like a bullet into a rabbit burrow that opened up miraculously in the bank before him. The terrible claws so close behind slashed harmlessly through empty air. The cat forced himself into the burrow as far as he could go, and crouched there, unable to turn and face what might come, for the burrow was very narrow. His pursuer, too, dropped to a crouching position, then pushed an exploratory paw into the burrow. The cat was fortunately out of reach, so the lynx lowered its head and rashly applied one malevolent green eye to the hole, withdrawing it quickly, however, and shaking the tawny ruffed head in baffled fury when a flurry of earth hit it full in the face — the cat's hind legs were working like pistons, hurling the earth back out of the hole.

The lynx drew back, to work out its next approach. Complete silence fell in the clearing, and all seemed peaceful and quiet in contrast to the wildly beating heart of the desperate, trapped cat.

Systematically the lynx began to dig away the earth around the entrance to the burrow with its powerful forepaws, and was so engrossed that it failed to hear, or to scent the soft downwind approach of a young boy wearing a bright red jacket and cap and carrying a rifle, who had entered the bush from the fields beyond. The boy was walking softly, not because he had seen the lynx, but because he was out after deer: he and his father, half a mile away, were walking in a parallel course, with pre-arranged signals, and the boy was very excited, for this was the first time his father had considered him responsible enough to accompany him with his own rifle. Suddenly he saw the infuriated animal scrabbling away at the earth, and heard it growling softly as a continuous hail of earth coming from an unseen source covered it. In that same instant the animal looked up and saw the boy It crouched low, snarling, and no fear showed in his eyes, only pure hatred. In a split-second decision, whether for fight or flight, it sprang; and in the same instant the boy raised his rifle, sighted and fired, all in one quick motion. The lynx somersaulted in the air and fell, its breath expelled in a mournful whistle as it hit the ground; the forelegs jerked once, a last spasm of nerves flickered across the fur, and it lay dead.

The boy was trembling slightly as he approached the dead animal, unable to forget the look of evil, savage fury on the catlike face which now lay before him, lips still curled back over white, perfect fangs. He stood looking down at his unexpected victim, unwilling to touch it, waiting for his father, who presently came, panting and anxious, calling as he ran. He stopped, staring at the tawny body lying on the pine needles, and then at the white face of his son.

He turned the animal over and showed the boy the small neat hole where the bullet had entered.

"Just below the breastbone." He looked up, grinning, and the boy smiled shakily.

The boy reloaded his rifle and tied his red neckerchief on a branch, marking the entrance to the clearing for their return. Then they walked off down the trail together, still talking, and the hidden cat heard their voices receding in the distance.

When all was silent he backed out of his refuge, and emerged into the sun-dappled clearing, his coat covered with sandy dirt. Completely ignoring the dead body even though forced to step around it, he sat down within ten yards of it, coolly washing his fur from the end of his tail to the tip of his nose. Then he stretched himself luxuriously, and with a final gesture of contempt turned his back on the lynx and dug into the earth with his hind claws to send a last shower of dirt over the animal's face. That done, he continued on his way, cool and assured as ever.

Two days later he caught up with the dogs. He came out on the crest of a hill forming one side of a valley, where a small stream meandered between alder-grown banks. Across the valley, clearly discernible among the bare trees on the opposite slope, he saw two familiar and beloved golden and white figures. His tail switched in excitement; he opened his mouth and uttered a plaintive, compelling howl. The two figures on the hill opposite stopped dead in their tracks, listening to the unbelievable sound as it echoed around the quiet valley. The cat leaped on to an overhanging rock, and as the hollow, raucous howl went ringing back and forth again the dogs turned questioningly, their eyes straining to seek the reality of the call. Then the young dog barked frenziedly in recognition and plunged down the hillside and across a stream, closely followed by the old dog. Now the cat began to run too, bounding like a mad thing down the hill, and they met on the banks of the little stream.

The old dog nearly went out of his mind with excitement: he covered the cat with frantic licking; twice he knocked him over with his eager thrusting head; then, carried away with enthusiasm, he started on the same tight intricate circles that he had used on the collie, whirling nearer and nearer until he finally burst free from the circle and rushed at the cat, who ran straight up the trunk of a tree, twisted in his own length, then dropped on the back of the dog below.

All through this performance the young dog had stood by, slowly and happily swinging his tail, his brown eyes alight and expressive, until at last his turn came when the old white clown collapsed in an ecstatic panting heap. Then the Labrador walked up to the cat, who rose on his hind legs, placing black forepaws on the neck of the great dog who towered above him, gently questing at the torn ear.

It would have been impossible to find three more contented animals that night. They lay curled closely together in a hollow filled with sweet-scented needles, under an aged, spreading balsam tree, near the banks of the stream. The old dog had his beloved cat, warm and purring between his paws again, and he snored in deep contentment. The young dog, their gently worried leader, had found his charge again. He could continue with a lighter heart.

9

OVER two hundred miles now lay behind them, and as a group they were whole and intact, but of the three only the cat remained unscathed. The old dog, however, still plodded cheerfully and uncomplainingly along. It was the Labrador who was in really poor condition: his once beautiful gleaming coat was harsh and staring now, his grotesquely swollen face in horrible contrast to his gaunt frame, and the pain in his infected jaw made it almost impossible for him to open his mouth, so that he was virtually starving. The other two now allowed him first access to any newly killed and bleeding animal provided by the cat, and he lived solely on the fresh blood that could be licked from the carcass.

They had slipped into a steady routine during the day; the two dogs trotting along side by side, unconcerned and purposeful, might have seemed two family pets out for a neighborhood ramble.

They were seen like this one morning by a timber-cruising forester returning to his jeep along an old tote road deep in the Ironmouth Range. They disappeared round a bend in the distance, and, pre-occupied with tree problems, he did not give them a second thought. It was with a considerable shock that he remembered them later on in the day, his mind now registering the fact that were was no human habitation within thirty miles. He told the senior forester, who roared with laughter, then asked him if he had seen any elves skipping around toadstools too?

But inevitably the time was drawing nearer when the disappearance of the animals must be uncovered, the hue and cry begin, and every glimpse or smallest piece of evidence be of value. The forester was able to turn the laugh a week later when his chance encounter was proved to be no dream.

At Heron Lake John Longridge and his brother were making plans for the last trip of the season. In England the excited Hunter family were packed in readiness for the voyage home. Mrs. Oakes was busy in the old stone house, cleaning and polishing, while her husband stacked the wood cellar.

Soon all concerned would be back where they belonged, like pieces of a jigsaw puzzle being fitted together; and soon it must be discovered that three of the pieces were missing. . . .

Sublimely unaware of the commotion and worry, tears and heartbreak that their absence would cause, the three continued on their way.

The countryside was less wild now, and once or twice they saw small lonely hamlets in the distance. The young dog resolutely avoided these, keeping always to the woods and dense bush wherever possible — much to the disgust of the old dog, who had implicit faith in the helpfulness and lovingkindness of human beings. But the young dog was the leader: however longingly the bull terrier looked towards a distant curl of smoke from a chimney he must turn away.

Late one afternoon they were followed for several miles by a single timber wolf who was probably curious about the cat and was no real menace: however hungry, it would never have risked an encounter with two dogs.

Like all his kind, however, the young dog hated and feared the wolf with some deep primeval instinct which must have had its origin in those mists of time when they shared a common ancestor. He was uneasy and disturbed by the slinking gray shape that merged into the undergrowth every time he looked back to snarl at it.

Unable to shake off the hateful shadow, and aware that the sun was sinking, irritable and exhausted with pain, he chose the lesser of two evils —leaving the bush for a quiet country road with small farms scattered at lonely intervals along it. He hurried his companions on, seeking protection for the night in the form of a barn or even an open field near a farm, sensing that the wolf would not follow within sight of human habitation.

They approached a small hamlet at dusk, a few small houses clustered around a schoolhouse and a white frame church. When the young dog would have skirted this too, the old terrier suddenly turned mutinous. He was, as usual, hungry; and the sight of the warm lights streaming out from the houses convinced him that this evening there was only one sensible way of obtaining food — from the hand of a human being! His eyes brightening at the thought, he ignored the young dog's warning growl, and trotted on unheeding down the forbidden road towards the houses, his rounded porcine quarters swinging defiantly, his ears laid back in stubborn disregard.

The young dog offered no further resistance. His whole head was throbbing violently with the pain of infection from the quills, and more than anything he wanted time to scratch and scratch, to rub the burning cheek along the ground.

The rebel passed the first few cottages, so snug and inviting to his comfort-loving soul — smoke rising in the still evening air, and the reassuring smell and sounds of humans everywhere. He paused before a small white cottage, snuffling ecstatically the wonderful aroma of cooking drifting out mingled with wood smoke. Licking his chops he walked up the steps, lifted a bold demanding paw and scratched at the door, then sat down, pricking his ears expectantly.

He was not disappointed. A widening stream of light from the opening door revealed a small girl.

The old dog grinned hideously in pleasure, his slanted eyes blinking strangely in the sudden light. There is little to equal a bull terrier's grin, however charmingly presented, for sheer astonishing ugliness.

There was a moment's silence, followed by an urgent wail of "Dad. . . ." Then the door slammed shut in his face. Puzzled but persistent, he scratched again, cocking his head to one side, his big triangular ears erect, listening to footsteps scurrying around within. A face appeared at the window. He barked a polite reminder. Suddenly the door was thrown open again and a man rushed out, a bucket of water in his hand, his face convulsed with fury. He hurled the water full in the face of the astonished dog, then grabbed a broom.

"Get out! Get out of here!" yelled the man, brandishing his broom so menacingly that the terrier tucked his tail between his legs and fled, soaking and miserable, towards his waiting companions. He was not afraid, only deeply offended — never in his long life had human beings reacted in such a way to his friendly overtures. Justifiable fury he knew and expected when he had terrorized their pets in the old days; laughter, and sometimes nervousness — but never a crude, uncivilized reception like this.

Baffled and disappointed, he fell meekly in behind his leader.

Two miles along the road they came to a winding cart track leading uphill to a farm. They crossed the dark fields, startling up an old white horse and some cows, heading for a group of outbuildings clustered together some distance from the farmhouse. A thin curl of smoke rose from the chimney of one. It was a smokehouse, where hams were smoking over a slow hickory fire. Pressing against the faint warmth at the base of the chimney they settled down for the night.

The young dog spent a restless night. The running sores on his face had been extended, by his continuous frantic clawing, into raw inflamed patches over the glands on one side of his neck; and the spreading infection was making him feverish and thirsty. Several times he left the others to drink from a small lake a short distance away, standing chest-deep in the cool, soothing water.

When the old dog woke shivering with cold he was alone. The cat was some distance away, belly to ground and tail twitching excitedly, stalking his breakfast. Stealing through the morning air came a familiar smell of smoke and something cooking — beckoning irresistibly.

The mists were rolling back from the valley, and a pale sun was lighting the sky when the old dog came through the windbreak of tall Norway pines and down outside the farmhouse door. His memory was short; already human beings were back on their rightful pedestals, cornucopias of dog food in their hands. He whined plaintively. At a second, louder whine, several cats appeared from the barn nearby and glared at him with tiger-eyed resentment. At any other time, he would have put them to instant flight; now he had more pressing business and chose to ignore them. The door swung open, a wondrous smell of bacon and eggs surged out, and the terrier drew up all the heavy artillery of his charm: with an ingratiating wag of his tail he glued his ears back, and wrinkled his nose in preparation for his disastrous winning leer. There was an astonished silence, broken by the deep, amused voice of a man. "Well!" said the owner of the voice, surveying his odd visitor, whose eyes were now rolled so far back that they had almost disappeared into his head. He called into the house, and was answered by the pleasant, warm voice of a woman. There was a sound of footsteps. The tail increased its tempo.

The woman stood for a moment in the doorway, looking down in silent astonishment at the white gargoyle on the step, and when he saw her face break into a smile that past master in the art of scrounging proffered a civil paw. She bent down and shook it, laughing helplessly, then invited him to follow her into the house.

Dignified, the old dog walked in, and gazed at the stove with bland confidence.

He was in luck this time, for there could not have been pleasanter people or a more welcoming house for miles around. They were an elderly couple, James Mackenzie and his wife Nell, living alone now in a big farmhouse which still held the atmosphere of a large, cheerful family living and laughing and growing up in it. They were well used to dogs, for there had been eight children in that house once upon a time, and a consequent succession of pets who had always started their adopted life out in the yard but invariable found their way into the household on the wildest pretexts of the children: misunderstood mongrels, orphaned kittens, sad strays, abandoned otter pups — Nell Mackenzie's soft heart had been as defenseless before them then as it was now.

She gave the visitor a bowl of scraps, which he bolted down in ravenous gulps, looking up then for more. "Why, he's starving!" she exclaimed in horror, and contributed her own breakfast. She petted and fussed over him, accepting him as though the years had rolled back and one of the children had brought home yet another half-starved stray. He basked in this affection, and emptied the bowl almost before it reached the ground. Without a word Mackenzie passed over his plate as well. Soon the toast was gone too, and a jug of milk; and at last, distended and happy, the old dog stretched out on a rug by the warmth of the stove while Nell cooked another breakfast.

"What is he?" she asked presently. "I've never seen anything quite so homely — he looks as though he had been squeezed into the wrong coat, somehow."

"He's an English bull," said her husband, "and a beauty too — a real old bruiser! I love them! He looks as though he'd been in a fight quite recently, yet he must be ten or eleven if he's a day!" And at the unqualified respect and admiration in the voice, so dear to the heart of a bull terrier — but so seldom forthcoming — the dog thumped his tail agreeably, then rose and thrust his bony head against his host's knee. Mackenzie looked down, chuckling appreciatively. "As cocksure as the devil — and as irresistible, aren't you? But what are we going to do with you?"

Nell passed her hand over the dog's shoulder and felt the scars, then examined them more closely. She looked up, suddenly puzzled. "These aren't from any dogfight," she said. "They're *claw* marks — like the ones bears leave on fresh wood, only smaller — "

In silence they looked down at the dog by their feet, digesting the implication, the unknown story behind the sinister scars; and they saw now, for the first time, the gathering cloudiness in the depths of the humorous little eyes; the too-thin neck shamed by the newly distended belly; and they saw that the indefatigable tail which thumped so happily on the floor was ragged and old, with a broken end. This was no bold, aggressive adventurer — only a weary old dog; hungry not only for food but for affection. There was no shadow of doubt in either what they would do — keep him, if he would stay, and give him what he needed.

They searched unavailingly under the white coat and in the pink ears for an identifying registered tattoo, then decided that when Mackenzie went into Deepwater to fetch some new churns later in the day he would make some inquiries there, tell the Provincial Police, and possibly put an advertisement

ın a city paper. And if nothing came of that . . .
"Then I guess we're landed with you for good, you
disreputable old hobo!" said Mackenzie cheerfully,
prodding his delighted audience with an experienced
foot, so that the dog rolled over on his back with a
blissful sigh and invited further attention under
his forearms.

When he opened the door that morning Mackenzie had seen a flight of mallards going down in the
direction of the small lake fed by the creek running
through the farm. It was still early enough to walk
over to see if they were still there, so he put a handful of shells in his pocket, took down an old pump
gun from the wall and set off, leaving Nell stepping
over and around the recumbent white form of their
guest as she cleared the table. He noticed that an
infinitesimal slit of eye followed her every movement.

Halfway over the still misty fields he stopped to
load his gun, then walked quietly toward the cover
of the alders fringing the little lake. Peering through
the branches, he saw six mallards about halfway
across, just out of range. With the wind the way
it was he might wait all day for a shot, unless something startled them on the other side.

But even as he turned away he saw a disturbance
in the reeds across the water. Simultaneously, quack-
ing loudly in alarm, the mallards took off in a body.
He fired twice as they came over, one bird plummet-
ing into the water and the other landing with a thud
on the shore nearby. He picked this one up, thinking

that he would have to bring the light canoe for the other, when he saw to his astonishment a large head of a dog swimming towards it.

The sound of a shot and the splash of a duck had had the same effect on the Labrador as a trumpet call to an old war horse, and drew him as irresistibly. Without a second's hesitation he had plunged in for the retrieve, only to find that he was unable to open his mouth to grasp the heavy duck properly, and was forced to tow it ashore by a wingtip. He emerged from the water twenty feet from the man, the beautiful greenhead trailing from its outstretched wing, the sun striking the iridescent plumage. The Labrador looked doubtfully at the stranger, and Mackenzie stared back in open-mouthed amazement. For a moment the two were frozen in a silent tableau, then the man recovered himself.

"Good dog!" he said quietly, holding out one hand. "Well done! Now bring it to me." The dog advanced hesitantly, dragging the bird.

"Give!" said Mackenzie, as the dog still hesitated.

The dog walked slowly forward, releasing his hold, and now Mackenzie saw with horror that one side of his face was swollen out of all proportion, the skin stretched so tautly that the eyes were mere slits and one rigid lip pulled back over the teeth. Sticking out like evil little pins on a rounded cushion of raw skin were several quills, deeply imbedded. Every rib showed up under the wet coat, and when the dog shook himself Mackenzie saw him stagger.

Mackenzie made up his mind quickly: no matter

whose, this dog was desperately in need of urgent treatment; the quills must be extracted at once before the infection spread further. He picked up the ducks, patted the dog's head reassuringly, then "Heel!" he said firmly. To his relief the dog fell in behind unquestioningly, following him back to the farmhouse, his resistance weakened to the point where he longed only to be back in the well-ordered world of human beings, that solid world where men commanded and dogs obeyed.

Crossing the fields, the stranger padding trustingly at his heels, Mackenzie suddenly remembered the other dog, and frowned in bewilderment. How many more unlikely dogs in need of succor would he lead into the farmhouse kitchen today — a lame poodle this afternoon, a halt beagle tonight?

His long, early morning shadow fell over the woodpile, and the sleepy Siamese cat sunning himself there lay camouflaged by stillness as he passed, unobserved by the man, but acknowledged by the dog with a brief movement of his tail and head.

Mackenzie finished cleaning up the Labrador's face nearly an hour later. He had extracted the quills with a pair of pliers; one had worked its way into the mouth and had to be removed from within, but the dog had not growled once, only whimpering when the pain was most intense, and had shown pathetic gratitude when it was over, trying to lick the man's hands. The relief must have been wonderful, for the punctures were now draining freely, and already the swelling was subsiding.

All through the operation the door leading out of the kitchen to a back room had shaken and rattled to the accompaniment of piteous whining. The old dog had been so much in the way when Mackenzie was working, pushing against his hand and obviously worried that they were going to do his companion some harm, that Nell had finally enticed him out with a bone, then quickly shut the door on his unsuspecting face.

Now, still deeply suspicious of foul play, he was hurling himself against the door with all his weight, but they did not want to let him in yet until the other dog had finished a bowl of milk. Mackenzie went to wash his hands, and his wife listened to the anxious running feet and the thuds that followed until she could bear it no longer, certain that he would harm himself. She opened the door and the old dog shot out in a fury, prepared to do battle on behalf of his friend — but he drew up all standing, a comical, puzzled expression on his face as he saw him peacefully lapping up a bowl of milk. Presently they sat down together by the door and the young dog patiently suffered the attentions of the other.

It was evident by their recognition and devotion that they came from the same home — a home which did not deserve to have them, as Nell said angrily, still upset by the gaunt travesty of a dog that had appeared; but Mackenzie pointed out that they must have known care and appreciation, as both had such friendly, assured dispositions. This made it all the harder to understand why they should be roaming such solitary and forbidding country, he admitted. But perhaps their owner had died, and they had run away together, or perhaps they had been lost from some car traveling across country, and were trying to make their way back to familiar territory. The possibilities were endless, and only one thing was certain — that they had been on the road long enough for scars to heal and quills to work their way inside a mouth; and long enough to know starvation.

"So they could have come from a hundred miles away or more," said Mackenzie. "From Manitoba, even. I wonder what they can have lived on, all that time — "

"Hunting? Scrounging at other farms? Stealing, perhaps?" suggested Nell, who had watched with amusement in the kitchen mirror her early morning visitor sliding a piece of bacon off a plate after breakfast when he thought her back was turned.

"Well, the pickings must have been pretty lean," said her husband thoughtfully. "The Labrador looks like a skeleton — he wouldn't have got much farther. I'll shut them in the stable when I go to Deepwater; we don't want them wandering off again. Now, Nell, are you quite sure that you want to take on two strange dogs? It may be a long time before they're traced — they may never be."

"I want them," she said simply, "for as long as they will stay. And in the meantime we must find something else to call them besides 'Hi!' or 'Good

dog.' I'll think of something while you're away," she added, "and I'll take some more milk out to the stable during the morning."

From his sunny observation post on the woodpile, the cat had watched Mackenzie cross the yard and usher the two dogs into a warm, sweet-smelling stable, shutting the door carefully behind him. Shortly afterwards the truck rattled down the farm road, then all was quiet again. A few curious farm cats were emboldened to approach the woodpile, resenting this exotic stranger who had taken possession of their favorite sunning place. The stranger was not fond of other cats at the best of times, even his own breed, and farm cats were beyond the pale altogether. He surveyed them balefully, considering his strategy. After two or three well-executed skirmishes the band dispersed, and the black-masked pirate returned to his lair to sleep.

Halfway through the morning he awoke, stretched, and jumped down, looking warily around before stalking over to the stable door. He bleated plaintively and was answered by a rustle of straw within. Leisurely, he gathered himself for a spring, then leaped effortlessly at the latch on the door. But he was not quite quick enough; the latch remained in position. Annoyed, unused to failure, he sprang again, this time making sure of success. For a split second, almost in the same impetus as the spring, one paw was curved around the wooden block handle supporting his weight, while the other paw released the latch above and the door swung open. Purring with restrained pleasure, the cat walked in, suffering a boisterous welcome from his old friend before investigating the empty bowl. Disappointed, he left the stable, the two dogs following him into the sunlit yard, and disappeared into the henhouse. Several enraged and squawking fowls rushed out as he made his way towards the nesting-boxes. Curving his paws expertly around a warm brown egg, he held it firmly, then cracked it with a neat sideways tap from a long incisor tooth, the contents settling intact on the straw. He had brought this art to perfection after years of egg stealing. He lapped with delicate unhurried thoroughness, helping himself to two more before retiring to his woodpile again.

When Mackenzie drove into the farmyard later on in the afternoon he was surprised to see the two dogs sleeping in the sun by the shelter of the cattle trough. They stood by the truck wagging their tails in recognition as he unloaded, then followed him into the farmhouse.

"Did you let them out of the stable, Nell?" he asked, opening a parcel at the kitchen table and sheepishly dropping a meaty bone into the shark-like mouth that had opened beside him.

"Of course not," she answered in surprise. "I took them out some milk, but I remember being particularly careful to close the door."

"Perhaps the latch wasn't down properly," said

Mackenzie. "Anyway, they're still here. The Lab's face looks better already — he'll be able to eat a decent meal by this evening, I hope; I'd like to get some meat on those bones."

Nothing was known of the runaways in Deepwater, he reported, but they must have come from the east, for a mink breeder at Archer Creek had spoken of chasing a white dog off his doorstep the night before, mistaking it for a local white mongrel well known for his thieving ways. Most men thought the Labrador could have been lost from a hunting trip, but nobody could account for an unlikely bull terrier as his companion. The Indian Agent had offered to take the Labrador if nobody turned up to claim him, as his own hunting dog had recently died. . . .

"Indeed he will not!" Nell broke in indignantly.

"All right," said her husband, laughing. "I told him we would never separate them, and of course we'll keep them as long as we can — I'd hate to think of one of my own dogs running loose at this time of year. But I warn you, Nell, that if they are heading somewhere with a purpose, nothing on earth will keep them here — even if they're dropping on their feet, the instinct will pull them on. All we can do is keep them shut in for a while and feed them up. Then, if they leave, at least we've given them a better start."

After supper that night the Mackenzies and their guests moved into the little back room: a cozy, pleasantly shabby place, its shelves still filled with children's books, tarnished trophies and photographs; while snowshoes, mounted fish and grandchildren's drawings jostled one another for space on the walls with award ribbons, pedigrees and a tomahawk. Mackenzie sat at a table, puffing peacefully on a pipe, and working at the minute, intricate rigging of a model schooner, while his wife read *Three Men in a Boat* aloud to him. The replete and satisfied Labrador had eaten ravenously that evening, cleaning up bowls of fresh milk and plates of food with a bottomless appetite. Now he lay stretched full length under the table in the deep sleep of exhaustion and security, and the terrier snored gently from the depths of an old leather sofa, his head pillowed on a cushion, four paws in the air.

The only disturbance during the evening was the noise of a tremendous cat battle out in the yard. Both dogs sat up immediately and, to the astonishment of the elderly couple watching, wagged their tails in unison, wearing almost identical expressions of pleased and doting interest.

Later on they followed Mackenzie out quite willingly to the stable, where he piled some hay in a corner of a loose box for them, filled the bowl with water, then shut the door firmly behind him — satisfying himself that the latch was down and firmly in place, and would remain so even when the door was rattled. Shortly afterwards the lights downstairs in the farmhouse went out, followed in a little while by the bedroom light upstairs.

The dogs lay quietly in the darkness, waiting.

Soon there was a soft scrabbling of paws on wood, the latch clicked, and the door opened a fraction, just enough to admit the slight body of the cat. He trampled and kneaded the hay for a while, purring in a deep rumble, before curling up in a ball at the old dog's chest. There were several contented sighs, then silence reigned in the stable.

When the young dog awoke in the cold hour before dawn only a few pale laggard stars were left to give the message which his heart already knew — it was time to go, time to press on westwards.

The yawning, stretching cat joined him at the stable door; then the old dog, shivering in the cold dawn wind; and for a few minutes the three sat motionless, listening, looking across the still dark farmyard, where already they could hear the slight stirrings of the animals. It was time to be gone: there were many miles to be traveled before the first halt in the warmth of the sun. Silently they crossed the yard and entered the fields leading to the dark, massed shadows of the trees in the farthermost corner, their paws making three sets of tracks in the light rime of frost that covered the field; and even as they turned onto a deer trail leading westward through the bush, a light came on upstairs in the farmhouse. . . .

Ahead of them lay the last fifty miles of the journey. It was as well that they had been fed and rested. Most of the way now lay through the Strellon Game Reserve, country that was more desolate and rugged than anything they had yet encountered. The nights would be frosty, the going perilous and exhausting; there could be no help expected from any human agency. Worst of all, their leader was already weak and unfit.

10

PIECES of a jigsaw puzzle were gradually joining together, and the picture was taking shape. In eastern Canada a liner was steaming up the St. Lawrence River, the heights of Quebec receding in the distance as she made her way to Montreal. Leaning against the railings on the upper deck, watching the panorama of the river, were the Hunters, returning from their long stay in England.

The children, Peter and Elizabeth, were wildly excited, and had hardly left the deck since the liner had entered the Gulf. Ever since they had wakened that morning, they had been counting the hours until their arrival home. There was all the joy and excitement of seeing their own homeland again, and soon their friends, their home and possessions — and above all they could not wait to see their pets. Over and over again Elizabeth had discussed their first meeting, for she was secretly longing to be reassured that Tao would not have forgotten her. She had bought him a red leather collar as a present.

Peter was perfectly happy and not in any way doubtful about his reunion; ever since he had been old enough to think at all he had known that, just as surely as Bodger belonged to him and was always there, so did he belong to the bull terrier — and his homecoming would be all the present that his dog would need.

And their father, seeing the endless arrowheads of mallards in the Canadian dawn, knew that soon he and the eager Luath would see them again, over the Delta marshlands and the stubble fields in the west. . . .

A thousand miles westward of the liner, John Longridge sat at his desk, a letter from his goddaughter in his hand, his thoughts as bleak as the empty, unresponsive house to which he had returned only a short while ago. He read the excited plans for her reunion with Tao — and of course the dogs — with a sinking heart, then laid the letter down unfinished, his despair deepening as he looked at the calendar: if the Hunters caught an early plane they would be home tomorrow night; in twenty-four hours' time he must give them his heartbreaking news — his charges were gone; and he had no idea where, or what had befallen them.

Mrs. Oakes was equally miserable. Between them

they had pieced together the fate of his charred note, and the course of confusion which had enabled three disparate animals to disappear without trace, and with perfect timing and perception. It was this perfection which had convinced him that his charges had not run away — if they had been unhappy, they could have gone at any time during the months of their stay.

He had already considered every possible catastrophe that could have overtaken them — death on the road, poison, traps, theft, disused wells — but not by the wildest stretch of imagination could he make any one of them account for three animals of such different temperaments. Nor could he understand how such a distinctive trio could pass unremarked in this small community: he had already spoken to some of Bodger's friends at the school, and not one sharp-eyed child had seen them that last morning, or any strange car, or in fact anything out of the ordinary; and Longridge knew that the area covered by rural school children was immense. The vast network of the Provincial Police could report nothing, either.

And yet he must have something more concrete than this to offer the Hunters tomorrow — if not a hope, at least a clear-cut finality.

He pressed his aching head into his hands and forced himself to set his thoughts out rationally: animals just did not vanish into thin air, so there must be some reasonable explanation for their disappearance, some clue as obvious and simple as the day-to-day pattern of their lives. A half-buried recollection stirred uneasily in his memory, but he could not identify it.

It was growing dark, and he switched on a lamp and moved over to light the fire. The silence in the room was oppressive. As he put a match to the kindling and watched the flames leap up, he thought of the last time he had sat by it: saw again a pair of dreaming sapphire eyes in their proud masked setting; tenanted his armchair with a luxuriously sprawling white form; and returned to the shadowy corner its listening, grieving ghost. . . .

Again the half-submerged memory distracted him: Luath's eyes . . . some difference in the pattern of his behavior . . . Luath's behavior on the last morning, the gesture of his unexpected paw . . . With a sudden flash of insight, he understood at last.

The door opened and he turned to Mrs. Oakes. "I know now — I know where they have gone," he said slowly. "Luath has taken them home — he has taken them all back to his own home!"

Mrs. Oakes looked at him in incredulous silence for a moment, then "No!" she burst out impulsively. "No — they couldn't do that! It's not possible — why, it must be nearly three hundred miles! And someone would have seen them — someone would have told us . . ." She broke off, dismayed, remembering that neither dog wore a collar. The terrier would carry no identifying marks, either, as he had been registered in England.

"They wouldn't be where anyone would see them," said Longridge thoughtfully. "Traveling by instinct, they would simply go west by the most direct route — straight across country, over the Ironmouth Range."

"Over the Ironmouth?" echoed Mrs. Oakes in horror. "Then there's no use hoping any more, if you're right," she said flatly. "There's bears and wolves and all manner of things, and if they weren't eaten up the first day they'd starve to death."

She looked so stricken and forlorn that Longridge suggested there was a good chance that they had been befriended by some remote prospector or hunter; perhaps, he enlarged, even now making his way to a telephone. . . .

But Mrs. Oakes was inconsolable.

"Don't let's fool ourselves any more, Mr. Longridge," she broke in. "I daresay a *young* dog could cross that country, and possibly even a cat — for there's nothing like a cat to look after itself — but you know as well as I do that old Bodger couldn't last ten miles! He used to be tired out after I'd walked him to my sister's and back. Oh, I know that half of it was put on to get something out of me," she admitted with a watery smile, catching Longridge's eye, "but it's a fact. No dog as old as that could go gallivanting across a wilderness and live for more than a day or two."

Her words fell away into a silence and they both looked out at the ominous dusk.

"You're right, Mrs. Oakes," said Longridge wearily at last. "We'll just have to face it — the old fellow is almost certainly dead. After all, it's been nearly four weeks. And I wouldn't give a candle for Tao's chances either," he added, "if we're going to be honest. Siamese can't stand the cold. But if they *did* make for their own home there's a chance at least that a big powerful dog like Luath would get there."

"That Luath!" said Mrs. Oakes darkly. "Leading that gentle old lamb to his death! And that unnatural cat egging him on, no doubt. Not that I ever had any favorites, but . . ."

The door shut, and Longridge knew that behind it she wept for them all.

Now that Longridge had his conviction to work on he wasted no time.

He called the Chief Ranger of Lands and Forests, and received assurance that word would be circulated throughout the department, and the game wardens and foresters contacted — tomorrow.

The Chief Ranger suggested calling a local bush pilot, who flew hunters into the remoter parts of the bush and knew most of the Indian guides.

The pilot was out on a trip and would not return until tomorrow; his wife suggested the editor of the rural section of the local newspaper.

The editor was still not back from covering a plowing match; his mother said that the hydro maintenance crew covered a large area of the country. . . .

The Line Superintendent said that he would be able to get in touch with the crews in the morning; he suggested the rural telephone supervisor, who was a clearinghouse of information for miles around. . . .

Everyone was sympathetic and helpful — but he was no farther on. He postponed the probable frustration of hearing that the supervisor would not be back from visiting her niece across the river until tomorrow, or that a storm had swept all the rural lines down, and searched for a map of the area.

He round a large-scale one, then drew a connecting line between his own small township and the university town where the Hunters lived, marking down the place names through which it passed. He found to his dismay that there were few of these, the line passing mostly through uninhabited regions of lakes and hills. The last forty or fifty miles seemed particularly grim and forbidding, most of it being in the Strellon Game Reserve. His hopes sank lower and lower, and he felt utterly despondent, bitterly regretting his offer to take the animals in the first place. If only he had kept quiet and minded his own business, they would all be alive now; for he was convinced, after looking at the map, that death through exposure, exhaustion, or starvation must have been inevitable.

And tomorrow the Hunters would be home again. . . . Dejectedly he picked up the phone and asked for the rural supervisor. . . .

Late that night the telephone rang. The telephone operator at Lintola — Longridge glanced at the map to find Lintola a good many miles south of his line — had some information: the schoolteacher had mentioned that the little Nurmi girl had rescued a half-drowned Siamese cat from the flooded River Keg, about two weeks ago, but it had disappeared again a few days afterwards. If Mr. Longridge would call Lintola 29 ring 4 tomorrow at noon she would try and have the child there and he could talk to her himself. The supervisor had one other piece of information which she offered rather diffidently for what it was worth — old Jeremy Aubyn, who lived up at the Doranda mine, had talked about "visitors" when he came in for his monthly mail collection, whereas everybody knew that the last visitor who had made the twelve-mile walk through the bush to the mine had been his brother, who had been dead for the last three years — poor old man. His only elaboration had been that they were "delightful people." . . . Old Mr. Aubyn had lived so long with only wild animals for company that he might easily be confused, she added delicately.

Longridge thanked her warmly, and put the receiver back, picking up the map. He discounted the information about the old recluse at the Doranda mine — who had probably met some prospectors or Indians — and concentrated on Lintola. It looked as though he had been right, then — they were indeed making for their own home. Two weeks ago, he puzzled, the cat had been alive, and, according to Longridge's map, must have traveled over a hundred miles. But what had happened to the other two? Must he now face the probability that Luath, too, was dead? Drowned possibly, as the cat would surely have been except for a little girl. . . .

Lying awake in the dark that night, unable to sleep, he thought that he would have given anything to feel the heavy thud on the bed that used to announce the old dog's arrival. How extremely unloving and intolerant he had felt so often, waking in the middle of the night to the relentless shoving and pushing of his undesirable and selfish bedfellow.

"Tonight," he reflected wryly, "I'd give him the whole bed! I'd even sleep in the basket myself — if only he would come back!"

11

LONGRIDGE'S hours of telephoning the night he returned had brought results; and in the following week he and the Hunters spent many hours patiently tracking down evidence which was sometimes so conflicting and confusing that it was useless, and sometimes so coincidental that it was difficult to believe. Sometimes they felt wearily that every man, woman or child who had seen a cat or a dog walking along a road in the last five years had called to tell them so. But on the whole everyone had been extraordinarily helpful and kind, and they had evidence of several genuine encounters. When the results had been sifted down, they bore out Longridge's original guess as to the line of travel — the dogs (nothing further had been heard of the cat) had taken an almost perfect compass course due west, and the line he had drawn on the map had been remarkably accurate.

The brother of one of the bush pilot's Indian

guides had met a cousin recently returned from rice harvesting who had some wild story of a cat and dog appearing out of the night and casting a spell over the rice crop so that it multiplied a thousand-fold; and the little girl called Helvi Nurmi, her voice distressed and tearful, had described in detail the beautiful Siamese cat who had stayed for so short a time with her. Somewhere in the Ironmouth Range a forester had reported seeing two dogs; and a surly farmer had been overheard in Joe Woods's General Store (Public Telephone), Philipville, saying that if he could lay hands on a certain white dog ("Ugly as sin he was — a great vicious powerful beast!") who had killed a flock of prize-winning chickens and savagely beaten up his poor peace-loving collie, he would break every bone in his body!

Peter had smiled for the first time on hearing this: it had conjured up for him a vivid picture of Bodger in his aggressive element, thoroughly enjoying himself in a fight, cheerfully wicked and unrepentant as ever. He would rather have heard this than anything, for he knew that his unquenchable, wayward old clown was not made for sadness or uncertainty. His deep grief he kept to himself, and would not undermine it now with this softening hope: Bodger was dead; Luath almost certainly so; and his conviction was steady and unalterable.

Elizabeth's attitude was the complete reverse of her brother's: she was completely and utterly convinced that her Tao was alive, and that sooner or later he would return. Nothing could shake her confidence, even though there had been no word of her cat since he had left the Nurmis' so long ago and so many miles away. She dismissed all tactful efforts to explain the odds against his return — someday, somehow, a penitent Siamese would re-appear, and, after a scolding due a thoughtless truant, he would receive with pleasure and surprise his new red collar. . . .

But she was the only one who held this cheerful confidence. After the kindly James Mackenzie had telephoned with the news that both dogs had been alive ten days ago, the family had pored over the map and seen the barrier that stretched between them and any admitted hope: wild, lonely terrain, rugged and cruel enough to beat down the endur-ance of any fresh and powerful dog, let alone the sick, half-starved, exhausted one that Mackenzie had described, leader and part sight for another whose willing heart could not withstand for long the be-trayal of his years. All that could be hoped for now was that the end of their journey had come quickly and mercifully in that wilderness.

Longridge was visting the Hunters; and, partly to get away from the depressing telephone calls from well-meaning but ill-informed people, and partly because it was Peter's twelfth birthday the follow-ing Sunday, he suggested that they all go and camp out in the Hunters' summer cottage on Lake Win-digo. Even though it had been closed for the winter, they could take sleeping bags, using only the living room and kitchen which could be warmed by the Quebec heater.

At first there had been some qualms from Elizabeth about leaving the house in case Tao should choose that week end to return, but Longridge showed her that Lake Windigo lay on the direct westward route that he had traced on the map, and reminded her that Tao knew the surrounding area for miles from his many expeditions with the dogs. Elizabeth packed the red collar and seemed satisfied — too easily, he suspected, dreading her disillusionment.

The cottage was full of memories, but it was easier to accustom the mind to new ones and train it to the loss in surroundings that were so different at this time of year. It was as if they were discovering new land; a cold lake empty of boats, the few cottages nearby all blindly shuttered, locked and empty. Trails that they did not even know existed were apparent, now that the trees were bare and the undergrowth had died down. Peter had a new camera, and spent hours stalking chipmunks, squirrels and birds with it. Elizabeth spent most of the days in a precarious treehouse they had built the previous summer between three great birches on the lake shore.

On the last afternoon, the Sunday of Peter's birthday, they decided to make a last expedition, taking the old Allen Lake Trail, then cutting off up the face of the hill to Lookout Point, and returning by the lake shore. It was an exhilarating walk through the crisp, clear air, the leaves thick and soft along the quiet trails, and over everything the indefinable healing peace and stillness of the northland bush.

They walked for the most part in companionable silence, each busy with his own thoughts. To Jim Hunter a walk without a dog lacked savor — and he remembered other fall days when, gun in hand, he had walked through this same peaceful solitude, Luath ranging from side to side: the excited summons to a treed partridge, and the gentleness of his dog's mouth around the soft fallen bird; then dawns and dusks on Manitoba marshes and lakes crowded his memory — freezing hours of patient waiting shared in canoes and blinds and stubble fields. The thought of Luath's last retrieve as Mackenzie had described it affected Hunter more than anything else; for he knew the frustrated humiliation his dog would feel with a pain-locked mouth and a bird to be brought in.

Peter had taken a short cut up the steep rockbound side of the hill. He sat on a log, staring into space, and he too remembered this time last year — when he had tried to train Bodger as a gun dog by throwing a stuffed leather glove into the bush after firing a BB gun: the willing co-operation and eager retrieves the first day; then, increasingly limp-tailed boredom and sulky ears, followed by deepening deafness, limping paws, and an unbearable air of martyrdom; and terminated two days running so subtly, by Bodger's appearance out of the bush with a diligent, puzzled expression — but no leather glove.

The corners of Peter's mouth lifted when he re-membered the scene that followed — the third day's throw and shot; then his quiet stalk after his White Hope into the depths of the bush — and the wily Bodger furiously digging a third glove grave. . . .

He sighed now — in his sudden loneliness rubbing his eyes with the back of his hand — and picked up his camera, for he could hear his family coming.

They sat for a long time on the flat rocks of the Lookout Hill, where long ago the Indians had built their warning signal fires, looking across the endless chains of lakes and tree-covered hills to the distant blur that was the great Lake Superior. It was very peaceful and quiet: a chickadee sang his poignant little piece for them, and the inevitable whisky-jack arrived on soundless wings to pick up cooky crumbs from within a few feet. Everyone was silent and pre-occupied.

Suddenly Elizabeth stood up.

"Listen!" she said. "Listen, Daddy — I can hear a dog barking!"

Complete and utter silence fell as everyone strained their ears in the direction of the hills be-hind. No one heard anything.

"You're imagining things," said her mother. "Or perhaps it was a fox. Come along, we must start back."

"Wait, wait! Just one minute — you'll be able to hear it in a minute, too," whispered Elizabeth, and her mother, remembering the child's hearing was still young and acute enough to hear the squeaking noise of bats and other noises lost forever to adults — and now even to Peter — remained silent.

Elizabeth's tense, listening expression changed to a slowly dawning smile. "It's Luath!" she announced matter-of-factly. "I know his bark!"

"Don't do this to us, Liz," said her father gently, disbelieving. "It's . . ."

Now Peter thought he heard something too: "Shhh . . ."

There was silence again, everyone straining to hear in an agony of suspense. Nothing was heard. But Elizabeth had been so convinced, the knowledge written so plainly on her face, that now Jim Hunter experienced a queer, urgent expectancy, every nerve in his body tingling with certain awareness that something was going to happen. He rose and hurried down the narrow path to where it joined the broader track leading around the hill. "Whistle, Dad!" said Peter breathlessly, behind him.

The sound rang out piercingly shrill and sweet, and almost before the echo rebounded a joyous, answering bark rang around the surrounding hills.

They stood there in the quiet afternoon, their taut bodies awaiting the relief of suspense; they stood at the road's end, waiting to welcome a weary traveler who had journeyed so far, with such faith, along it. They had not long to wait.

Hurtling through the bushes on the high hillside of the trail a small, black-tipped wheaten body leaped the last six feet down with careless grace and landed softly at their feet. The unearthly, discordant wail of a welcoming Siamese rent the air.

Elizabeth's face was radiant with joy. She kneeled, and picked up the ecstatic, purring cat. "Oh, Tao!" she said softly, and as she gathered him into her arms he wound his black needle-tipped paws lovingly around her neck. "Tao!" she whispered, burying her nose in his soft, thyme-scented fur, and Tao tightened his grip in such an ecstasy of love that Elizabeth nearly choked.

Longridge had never thought of himself as being a particularly emotional man, but when the Labrador appeared an instant later, a gaunt, stare-coated shadow of the beautiful dog he had last seen, running as fast as his legs would carry him towards his master, all his soul shining out of sunken eyes, he felt a lump in his throat, and at the strange, inarticulate half-strangled noises that issued from the dog when he leaped at his master, and the expression of his friend's face, he had to turn away and pretend to loosen Tao's too loving paws.

Minutes passed; everyone had burst out talking and chattering excitedly, gathered around the dog to stroke and pat and reassure, until he too threw every vestige of restraint to the winds, and barked as if he would never stop, shivering violently, his eyes alight and alive once more and never leaving his master's face. The cat, on Elizabeth's shoulder, joined in with raucous howls; everyone laughed, talked or cried at once, and for a while there was pandemonium in the quiet wood.

Then, suddenly — as though the same thought had struck them all simultaneously — there was silence. No one dared to look at Peter. He was standing aside, aimlessly cracking a twig over and over again until it became a limp ribbon in his hands. He had not touched Luath, and turned away now, when the dog at last came over including him in an almost human round of greeting.

"I'm glad he's back, Dad," was all he said. "And your old Taocat, too!" he added to Elizabeth, with a difficult smile. Elizabeth, the factual, the matter-of-fact, burst into tears. Peter scratched Tao behind the ears, awkward, embarrassed. "I didn't expect anything else — I told you that. I tell you what," the boy continued, with a desperate cheerfulness, avoiding the eyes of his family, "You go on down — I'll catch up with you later. I want to go back to the Lookout and see if I can get a decent picture of that whisky-jack." There will never be a more blurred picture of a whisky-jack, said Uncle John grimly to himself. On an impulse he spoke aloud.

"How about if I came too, Peter? I could throw the crumbs and perhaps bring the bird nearer?" Even as he spoke he could have bitten back the words, expecting a rebuff, but to his surprise the boy accepted his offer.

They watched the rest of the family wending their way down the trail, Tao still clutched in

Elizabeth's arms, gentle worshiping Luath restored at last to the longed-for position at his master's heels.

The two remaining now returned to Lookout Point. They took some photographs. They prised an odd-shaped fungus growth off a tree. They found, incredibly, the cylindrical core of a diamond drill. And all the time they talked: they talked of rockets, orbits, space; gravely they pondered the seven stomachs of a cow; tomorrow's weather; but neither mentioned dogs.

Now, still talking, they were back at the fork of the trail; Longridge looked surreptitiously at his watch: it was time to go. He looked at Peter. "We'd better g — " he started to say, but his voice trailed off as he saw the expression on the face of the tense, still frozen boy beside him, then followed the direction of his gaze. . . .

Down the trail, out of the darkness of the bush and into the light of the slanting bars of sunlight, joggling along with his peculiar nautical roll, came — Ch. Boroughcastle Brigadier of Doune.

Boroughcastle Brigadier's ragged banner of a tail streamed out behind him, his battle-scarred ears were upright and forward, and his noble pink and black nose twitched, straining to encompass all that his short peering gaze was denied. Thin and tired, hopeful, happy — and hungry, his remarkable face alight with expectation — the old warrior was returning from the wilderness. Bodger, beautiful for once, was coming as fast as he could.

He broke into a run, faster and faster, until the

years fell away, and he hurled himself towards Peter.

And as he had never run before, as though he would outdistance time, Peter was running towards his dog.

John Longridge turned away, then, and left them, an indistinguishable tangle of boy and dog, in a world of their own making. He started down the trail as in a dream, his eyes unseeing.

Halfway down he became aware of a small animal running at lightning speed towards him. It swerved past his legs with an agile twist and he caught a brief glimpse of a black-masked face and a long black tail before it disappeared up the trail in the swiftness of a second.

It was Tao, returning for his old friend, that they might end their journey together.

You have just finished reading a wonderful book by a master storyteller. If you enjoyed it or if you were moved by it, may we suggest you share your experience and recommend THE INCREDIBLE JOURNEY to a friend.

ABOUT THE AUTHOR

SHEILA BURNFORD was born in Scotland and attended St. Georges and Harrogate College. She has contributed to PUNCH, CANADIAN POETRY and the GLASGOW HERALD. *THE INCREDIBLE JOURNEY* was her first book. Since then she has written *The Fields of Noon* and *Without Reserve*. She now lives with her husband and family in Port Arthur, Ontario.